EVELYN CONLON

MOVING ABOUT THE PLACE

·THE· BLACK -STAFF PRESS

First published in 2021 by Blackstaff Press
an imprint of Colourpoint Creative Ltd
Colourpoint House
Jubilee Business Park
21 Jubilee Road
Newtownards BT23 4YH

With the assistance of the Arts Council of Northern Ireland

Printed by GPS Colour Graphics Ltd, Belfast

A CIP catalogue record for this book is available from the British Library

ISBN 978 1 78073 310 4

www.blackstaffpress.com

For those who kept the heads open;
friends here, there and everywhere.

Contents

The Meaning of Missing

I think of the feeling around a person being missing as being a narrow thing. It has to be, in order to get into so many places. I told my husband this once and he laughed at me.

'Well, if you can think of heartbreak as a thin piercing agony ...' I began again.

He said that the turnips needed thinning, and that he was away out to the garden. He didn't like talking about heartbreak, because he had once caused it to me by going off to live a new life for three months. It obviously didn't work out because he turned up on my doorstep on Thursday, 6 June, twenty years ago. At ten past eight. Evening. He wasn't contrite, just chastened. He has been here since, but he never talks about that time. I don't mind too much, because I never admitted that I had cried crossing every bridge in Dublin, the only way to get to know a city I was told by someone who was clearly trying to get me away from her doorstep. Go down to the river, it will be good for you. Nor did I admit to what I'd done as soon as the crying had dried up and all the bridges had been crossed. I didn't have to, and he couldn't really ask me or hold me accountable.

Thinning turnips, ha! You'd think we had an acre out the back, and that he was going to have to tie old hot-water bottles around his knees because the length of time on the ground was going to be so hard on them. We have one drill of turnips, a half of cabbage and a half of broad beans. Although it's not strictly an economical use of the space, I insist on the broad beans, because of the feel of the inside of them. Only two drills. They could have waited. Of course, he didn't like me talking about missing either. That's about my sister.

'She's not missing,' my husband insisted. 'You've just not heard from her.'

I often replay my conversations with him as if he is standing right beside me. I bet I'll be able to do that if he dies before me.

'For a year!'

'Yes, for a year. But you know how time goes when you're away.'

I don't actually. I've never been away for a year. Nor for three months.

When my sister said she was going to Australia there was a moment's silence between us, during which time a little lump came out of my heart and jumped into my stomach. We were having our second glass of Heineken. In deference to the scared part of our youth, when we were afraid to be too adventurous, she always drank Heineken when out with me. She didn't want to hold the predictability of my life up to the light. I knew that she had gone through ten different favourite drinks since those days, none of them Heineken.

'Australia!' I squealed.

2

I coughed my voice down.

'Australia?' I said, a second time, in a more melodious tone. Strange how the same word can mean two different things when the pitch is changed. Béarla as Chinese. I must have hit the right note, curious but not panicked, because she smiled and said yes. Not only was she going, she had everything ready, tickets bought, visa got. She might even have started packing for all I know. It was the secret preparation that rankled most. How could she have done those things without telling me? If we were going to Waterford for a winter break, I'd tell her weeks in advance.

The day she left was beautifully frosty. She stayed with us the night before, and after I had gone to bed, I could hear her and my husband surfing for hours on a swell of mumbling and laughing. Apparently, she was too excited to go to sleep and he decided to get in on the act, not often having an excited woman to lead him into the small hours. The morning radio news said that if there was an earthquake in the Canaries, Ireland might only have two hours to prepare for a tsunami. Brilliant – another thing to worry about. And us just after buying a house in Skerries.

At the airport, my emotions spluttered, faded, then surged again, like a fire of damp coal. The effort involved in not crying stiffened my face, and yet it twitched, as if palsy had shot into a line from my forehead to my chin. But I was determined. I would keep my dignity, even if the effort was going to paralyse me. It would be an essential thing to have, this dignity, now that I was not going to have a sister. My husband touched my shoulder as we got back into the car, because he can do that sometimes, the right thing.

In the months that followed I mourned her in places that I had never noticed before, and in moods that I had not known existed. First there is presence and then it has to grow into absence. There are all sorts of ways for it to do that, gently, unnoticeably, becoming a quiet rounded cloud that complements the sun with its dashing about, making harmless shadows. Or the other way, darkly with thunder.

'It's not as if you saw her all the time,' my husband said, unhelpfully.

'I did,' I said back.

'What are you talking about? You only met every few months.'

'But she was there.'

She wrote well, often referring to the minutiae of her journey. But no matter how frequently she talked about cramped legs or the heat in Singapore, and despite the fact that I'd seen her off at the airport myself, I still imagined her queuing for a ship at Southampton, sailing the seas for a month, having dinner in prearranged sittings at the sound of a bell, because that's the way I would have done it.

And then she stopped writing, fell out of touch, off the world. My letters went unanswered, her telephone was cut off. I'm afraid, because my pride was so riled, the trail was completely cold by the time I took her real missing seriously. And still my husband insisted that there was nothing wrong with her, just absent-mindedness.

Time passed. I didn't wonder about her all day every day. Not all day.

I was in bed sick when she rang. I love the trimmings of being sick, mainly the television at the bottom of the bed, although after two days I was getting a little TV'd out. I had just seen John Stalker, a former chief of police in England advertising garden awnings. I was puzzled as to why they gave his full title. Did the police thing have anything to do with awnings? Was there a pun there, hidden from

4

me? I didn't like being confused by advertisements. If I'd had a remote control, I could have switched the volume down occasionally and lip-read the modern world. Then *Countdown* came on. Making up the words made me feel useful. I had seen the mathematician wearing that dress before. It was during the conundrum that the phone rang; it wasn't a crucial conundrum, because one of the fellows was streets ahead of the other – even I had him beaten hands down and I had a temperature of 100 degrees or thereabouts.

'Hello, hello.'

And there was her voice, brazen as all hell got up. Her actual voice. I straightened myself against the headboard and thought, 'It's the temperature.' I straightened myself more and my heart thumped very hard. It sounded like someone rapping a door. I thought it would cut off my breathing.

'Hi,' she said.

'Hello,' I said, as best as I could manage.

'Oh my God, it's been soooo long …'

The sentence sounded ridiculous and the stretched-out word was, frankly, juvenile.

'… and I'm really sorry about that. But I'll make up for it. I'm on my way back for a few weeks. I'll be arriving on Saturday morning.'

Back. Not home. Well, Saturday didn't suit me, and even if it had up until this moment, it suddenly wasn't going to. I was speechless, truly. My mind was working overtime, dealing with silent words tumbling about. I could almost hear them scurrying around, looking for their place in the open. What would be the best way to get revenge?

She must have finally noticed because she asked, 'Are you there?'

'Oh yes,' I said.

Short as that, 'Oh yes.'

I don't think I said more than ten words before limping to a satisfactorily oblique fade-out.

'See you. Then.'

I put the phone down, my hand shaking. How many people had I told? And would I have to tell them all that she was no longer missing? And had I also told them about my husband's view? And was he now right? If a person turns up have they ever been missing? How could I possibly remember what conversations I had set up or slipped into casually, over the past year. I hoped that my sister would have a horrible flight, bumpy, stormy, crowded, delayed. But that's as far as my bile could flower.

My husband went to the airport. He would, having no sense of the insult of missing. He fitted the journey in around the bits and pieces of a Saturday, not wanting me to see him set out, not wanting to leave the house under the glare of my disapproval.

By evening I had mellowed a little because I had to. It was seeing her, the shape of her, the stance of her as she leaned against the kitchen table, the expressions of her. My sister had never giggled, even in the years that are set aside for that. She had always had a touch of wry. Getting ready for her life, no doubt, away ahead of me, I thought, always ahead of me. On the third evening, by the time the ice in my chest had begun to melt, the three of us went out to our local.

'What's Wollongong like?' I asked.

'Just a normal Australian town,' my sister said, and shrugged loudly, if that is possible. And then she mercilessly changed the subject. I had thought it would have jacaranda trees in bloom all year, birds calling so busily that it would be the first thing a person would mention, as a writer once did, sun flitting continuously on the sparkling windows of every house. A town rampant with light. I had thought it a place for rumination, with colour bouncing unforgettably off the collocation of gum trees.

'Are you sure it's just a normal town. Have you been there?'

'Yes, totally normal. Of course I've been there.'

I didn't believe her for one second.

'Why do you particularly want to know what Wollongong is like?'

'The name,' my husband said, as if he was my ventriloquist. But something in my demeanour made him hesitate, and he looked at me as if he had made some mistake.

'It's just that I met someone from there,' I said.

'When?' they both asked. Normally my sister and my husband have a murmuring familiarity between them, born presumptuously of their relationship with me. But they were suddenly quiet, each afraid to admit that they did not know when I, I of the dried-up life, would have met someone from Wollongong. Was it during her year or his three months? Damn, they would be thinking, now they each knew that the other didn't know. And me sitting there smiling away to myself. Smug, they would have been surmising. But I wasn't smug. I admit to a moment of glee, but I was mostly thinking of Wollongong, and I swallowed the sliver of triumph because I am known for my capacity to forgive.

However, I didn't answer the question and went to the bar to buy my round, feeling like a racehorse, unexpectedly out in front, showing the rest of the field a clear set of hooves.

Two Gallants Getting Caught

It was a fairly beautiful morning, not stunning or anything like that, but passable for September in Dublin. The usual finger-wagging mist was hanging about but there was an occasional chink in the grey, a small curtain being parted coquettishly to show what was up above. The sky was threatening to come out. If you had never seen continuous cerulean you would have thought the whole day all right.

Two boyos, one called Lenehan and the other Corley, turned in their beds. One of them vaguely wondered about last night and what had happened to give him this twinge of uneasiness with himself, but the turning over tumbled him happily from self-examination back into sleep.

The participants at the conference, reluctantly called *Another Look at Joyce*, collected their various bits and pieces, assembled themselves as best they could, and trooped out on to the streets of Dublin to make their way to Trinity College. Some people knew every name of every street;

others had declined that route. They were off to make sense of things through looking at writers and what they might have meant, and how the dead ones stood up or didn't. This was as good a way of making sense of the world as, say, business is, or prayer.

Mind you, it depends on who is leading the prayers, Ruth thought, as she got ready to ascend the steps, talking to herself quite legibly. A woman needs to be able to do that, round out her thoughts without interruption; it might be her only defence against what's in store for her. L'esprit de l'escalier can be overrated; what you think is more important than what you say. She knew that: she'd had to fight for every inch of intelligent space as most of those around her did their very best to dirty her brain with small talk and small views of herself. She'd looked at conversations that she was being forced into and she'd seen them metamorphose into mouths that were chewing and spitting out her dreams.

Toby Doyle took the steps, sometimes two at a time, behind her. He could afford to miss the occasional one. He had just caught sight of that Ruth and wanted to almost catch up with her; he'd heard that she had new things to say. As he hurried to get closer to her, a shadow from the past walked straight at him, never ducked, straight at him, aiming to go through him. It blacked out the scrap of sun that was trying to blossom. Shivering, he steadied himself, so as not to become mesmerised by the brief bit of dark cast on the stone. At the same moment Ruth felt an invisible breath kiss her face. She touched her cheek.

The two boyos had begun their walk down the slight hill of Rutland Square; Lenehan had done his first resentful jump down off the footpath.

The delegates entered the hall, gave some mild greetings to colleagues – Ruth to Peggy and that Italian woman; Toby to Joseph and to him from Princeton. No one took offence at any noticeable lukewarmth; they were used to this level of distraction. Ruth sat down where she could see one of the few windows. A couple of drops of old rain slid down it. Toby sat on the raised seat two rows behind her. Lachey sidled in beside him. Other delegates shuffled or bent, then sat; the occasional one jauntily threw a leg over a knee. They took out notebooks or, in the case of some, the latest iBook. A few stared straight ahead as if they were somewhere else. An awful lot was going on today; they had much to say, much to argue, rows to stoke and conclusions to hint at. And choices had to be made as to which conflicting papers to attend. Now this was a real dilemma. It might seem harmless enough from the gods above but it was not, it was not, and required some thought, and then changing of mind after more thought. There were those who could take these decisions with humour and there were those who could not. The plenary paper of the day had started. All hands got on deck, and in no time at all it was time for coffee.

'I see you're talking about "Two Gallants". Bit of a leap for you,' a tall rangy man said to a corpulent one. They were surrounded by men in various shades of in-between.

'I'm going to that,' the suddenly-animated Italian woman said in an olive voice. After all, she could like the way Joyce painted the men: she was in no competition with that, her way of seeing them was not much different to his. The ceiling of her own sky had maybe helped him view them. And he had liked women, in his way, had the nerve of a woman in places, had what it took to face down men who were lesser than his own Nora. He had sat at a window in Trieste, just as D.H. Lawrence had later looked out at Gargnano and carved the dirt of the mines, while the diamond light of Lombardy poured from the sky around him. From Piazza Ponterosso, Joyce walked Dublin, doing his best to brush aside the cataracts of nostalgia. It was while swallowing a mouthful of wine, and drawing perfect smoke into his lungs, that Lenehan and Corley jumped out at him on the street corner of either city and said *go on, sharpen your nib, write us then if you're so good. They surprised him really. He'd been thinking of how dry the sun here seemed, when all of a sudden he saw Corley sneaking behind Lenehan, eyeing up the girl. He saw him move into the cafe and sullenly swallow his distaste. And he saw everything in between. Go on, write about us, describe us if you can. Between Rutland and Ponterosso, where the domestic sounds mixed with the smell of love, Lenehan had a moment of thought. He thought about changing his shape, like a fox might in the middle of the night. He could have become gallant. But that would have taken a lot of work. Easy, Mr Joyce, that was not fair. The city may seem small to you now that you're looking out on a via, but remember all that walking that has to be done, the miles between the cigarettes. Lenehan was out of his own hands now. Oh well, whatever you think. We'll get our own back, we'll get the backroom boys to refuse to print – after all Corley talks to policemen.*

The page flickered on the shadow of a casa.

'What!' the tall man bellowed, looking down at Rosa Maria, 'You're going to that? I would have thought you'd hate them.'

'Why?' Rosa Maria asked, looking up at him with one eyebrow higher than the other. Her hair was black, her face illumined with enjoyment.

'Well …' There was a trap here somewhere but he couldn't find it.

'Ah, but I like the way they were imagined. I could hate them but I don't,' she said, her eyes crinkling at the corners, letting him off, saving his fall.

'I see,' Toby said, from the left-hand side of the circle, not seeing at all. A woman pushed a tea cart on the outskirts and started collecting cups.

The two boyos were making good headway to take their places in Sackville Street amongst the crowd, the crowd that moved this way and that, making space for them as if they were joining a Sunday evening choir. Those two streets they'd just graced could be named for heroes.

Sessions 1, 2 and 3 were about to start, so Ruth rushed away from her coffee and made her way to Room 1904, followed closely by Toby Doyle, who had not until that moment known which choice he was going to make. The man who took to the podium was, surprisingly, every bit as good-looking as the picture on the programme, maybe even better. His hair fell down in tresses around his eyes and he coughed slightly when everyone was seated. He brushed the table with his hand, then looked straight at the audience.

'Patrick Kavanagh was right,' he said, in a surprisingly deep voice. Ruth would have expected polished slimness in it.

'He was right about Who killed James Joyce?/ I, said the commentator,/ I killed James Joyce/ For my graduation.

'And he was right about What weapon was used/ To slay mighty Ulysses?/ The weapon that was used/ Was a Harvard thesis.

'But particularly he was right about Who carried the coffin out?/ Six Dublin codgers/ Led into Langham Place/

By W.R. Rodgers.'

A laugh went up and people settled themselves nicely; they'd be able to tuck into this paper. It would certainly make a change from the last one, which was given by a scholar who had translated *Finnegans Wake* into Catalan. 'As if you should,' said the introducer, causing a deep frown to move over the face of the speaker. And it had never lifted. Then, how could it, thought Ruth sympathetically; if you'd done all that work and a juvenile speaker could get up and throw that line out of a hangover, you too would keep a frown on your face and heart. But it looked like this curly-headed chap would entertain them.

'I do not intend to become the unwritten verse in Kavanagh's poem. I do not. You are wondering how I will achieve that; well, this is how ...'

And he lifted his single sheet of paper, walked off the podium and out the door. The participants watched him go, laughed again and waited for him to return. The realisation that he was not going to come back dawned on some people sooner than others. A choice now had to be made, whether to continue laughing or get indignant.

'Well, that's one way of getting out of it if you've nothing prepared,' Ruth said, breaking the silence. Toby Doyle wished he'd thought of that. She got up to leave and others shifted to follow her. Some made to call in late to other sessions, deciding along the way whether to mention their smart-arse, or whether to annoy him by not referring to it at all. Ruth made for the door, deciding to get some unexpected fresh air.

Lenehan slipped out on to the road to look up at the blue Trinity clock; it was always reliable. He thought the 'always' superfluous, but there you go.

Corley said, I always let her wait a bit, sweating that this might be just the time she would decide to move forward, decide that the petting of his ego and the mediocre kissing was just not worth the humiliation of having to stand on a street corner, pretending to be excited by the thoughts of him. Funny that men dressed like him were never good at kissing. Him and his oily head.

As Ruth walked around the fence, she saw Stephen in the distance. She'd slept with him once. You could do that now without fear of getting caught, if so minded, thanks to Carl Djerassi and his cohorts, who devised a pill, known as the pill. No one here might know their names, silly them. The women these men knew must have helped them, tried out their ideas even, made sure that Ruth now had the means not to get caught. She remembered Stephen as a startled lover, a man you could want as a friend.

The touch of the rails on her fingers made her hands hot with history.

There was no cockiness about her, but there was something, a hidden pride for being here in this place, it was in all the secret pockets of her. Her grandmother had worked as a housemaid, for priests, doctors and the like. Ruth had only just found out things about her life, for who cared what happened to the girl in the basement. Ruth walked up Grafton Street, took a detour as far as the Conservatory of Music on Chatham Row, past the pub where she'd had a drink last night. She walked by a room where a recital was being prepared. A man was in battle with his own capabilities, eyes occasionally closed to shut out any sense that would interfere. A woman sat turning the pages, perfectly in time; she too must have known the notes. A shot of Puccini wafted out through the opened window – a pigeon got carried away with it and flew into the glass, momentarily stunning itself. It lifted its wing and passed it over its blushing eyes in order to forget the mistake it had made, just like a cat would. Ruth smiled. Now who's lucky, she thought, because she was prone to optimism. She should go back now, it was time for the next movement into the understanding of why artists do what they do, and how.

The two boyos had passed the almost naked harp. The music had come whispered to them, like something running underwater waiting for its moment to emerge.

It was time for Sessions 4, 5 and 6. Number 6 was Ruth's.

Paper 2 in Session 4 was being given by Toby Doyle himself. He was now thought of as TD. As the coffee-break conversation prepared to fall into an echo and the woman on the outskirts rattled the cups, his grin got wider; it covered the entire bottom of his face now, even falling down into his chin. He straightened himself up and took on a priestly stance. He was pleased with himself. You see he had it figured out. It required a lot of work to do a paper on Joyce. You couldn't just talk about yourself and him, and the effect he'd had on you, or at least the effect you thought he ought to have had on you. All that had been done before, hundreds of times, by people with higher opinions of their own thoughts. But he had it nailed. This time he had really nailed it. He had paid Lachey to trawl the most obscure papers given in the most obscure places and he had rearranged them to fit into his own experience. Getting Lachey to do this had been easy enough. The conversation had gone something like: 'I couldn't do that. How much? Good lord, all right.'

TD was an expert at this; he knew just how much of what to pay in order to get the evening swinging his way. It didn't always have to be money, it could be another currency, a good word dropped here and there, a bad word dropped accidentally. Hadn't he got a quote of his, among the poets, on the entrance to the labour ward – how else except by some words or deeds somewhere? The fact that there were women who wanted to change their maternity hospital after looking at it during a number of long waits was neither here nor there to him. He smiled some more: today was going to be good. He knew how to read Joyce, not everyone did. There were some people who thought that you could decipher it in different ways. He didn't agree – he thought you had to be a particular kind of man to understand *Finnegans Wake*. Woman? Ah no, he didn't think so. But the funny thing was, sometimes, just sometimes … For instance, he'd like to get close to that Ruth, converse with her, debate some things with her … all right, copy some of her notes, if the opportunity presented itself. That way he'd get a new view, because surely, she wouldn't have the same thoughts as the rest of the panels. She didn't look as if she would, something about her. She would surely have a fresh and pearly thing to say.

Now there was a thought, if he could find Lachey again. Very few people would go to her paper and certainly no one would go to both hers and his, so if he just got the gist of her points, he could pass it off easily enough as his own in the summing-up paper he had to do for the closing session. Hadn't he managed similar before without notice? Once, he'd had a bit of a scare. Some mad woman claimed that he'd taken her essay 'The Shades of *Yonnondio* in *The Grapes of Wrath*' and used the entire premise of it. He'd laughed it off of course, snorting, who on earth could think that he'd have even heard of the publication, whatever the name of it was. Naturally everyone believed him. (He'd found the obscure review in the sitting room of a woman he'd slept with, he was nearly sure.)

'I don't like stealing from a girl,' Lachey said.

'If you're worried about being found out, remember that if you stole from a man, chances are someone might have heard it before, but a girl, it's unlikely. You'll never be caught,' TD reassured him.

'That's a terrible thing to say,' Lachey replied.

'Oh, there's been worse said, believe me, and will be again. Go,' and Lachey remembered favours given and still needed.

TD looked across the delegates who were gathering themselves together again, dropping their thoughts into their own particular expertise. He smiled at Ruth, she half smiled back, a bit disdainfully he thought. Well, wait until she found that only six people were going to her paper and over a hundred to his.

However, that is not what happened.

Lenehan let his hand run along the railings of Duke's Lawn. Look at it, standing there between the Museum and the Library, it could definitely make a good home for a parliament. Wouldn't that be something new.

The delegates moved en bloc to hear Ruth's paper. She stood in the same spot as the Catalan translator and the Kavanagh lover, who hadn't been seen since, and began.

'Good afternoon and thank you for your presence. I know that it can be difficult to decide what are the new things we need to know about Joyce. And I may be about to add to those difficulties because I'm here to tell you that the slavey in the Baggot Street house was a real person and, while that might not discommode the work of everyone, it may cause upset to some. The slavey was my grandmother. I have recently been given a letter, found by a diligent librarian among the bits and pieces gone yellow at the bottom of a box belonging to several women, hard to say what belonged to what one. Not much fuss about that then. But the librarian noticed the address and names and sent the letter on to me, for which I am grateful. She was of the opinion that these things matter, particularly when all concerned are dead.'

Ruth turned the page for the audience to see. The writing was slanted to the left, lying back, looking expectantly up to the top of the page.

Dear Eve, I will not tell you everything that happened to-day because to-day was no different than any other day, how could it be, but there was one thing last week. I'll get to that later. I did the usual pot walloping in the kitchen, the usual bed making, the usual emptying, dusting, scrubbing. I tried that thing you used to do to rub the pain from my back and knees. But I still like the house, I like walking about it. I pass the mistress with no sadness in my eyes. They assume that because I'm a maid I was born to be a maid. And that I think like a maid. They love knowing that, although they don't know what a maid thinks like. They do not know that a girl proficient in scrubbing and emptying their chamber pots would have an ambition or two worked out, as well as the way to achieve it. I do hope that your new place is as good and not as bad as here. It will only be for a short time now with your marriage coming so soon. I thought of you the other night when I was getting ready for bed. I know that you were worried about me going to meet the Corley boy, such an idea that he had that we wouldn't find out his name. But you know I always told you that I was well able for him and that the journey on the tram to Donnybrook was something to look forward to. It was worth putting up with his swagger for the interest of it. And he was always nice enough. I didn't even mind him asking me to get him a bit of money if I could. I should have minded but I didn't. The first time he was so grateful. But he never mentioned it the next time and he then put the squeeze on me again. I didn't like that. Not one bit. So last Sunday I was to meet him but I went for a walk with the other maid first, the one from your part of the country, and there he was deep in talk with a friend of his. Both of them were engrossed, so I walked behind them for a bit, luckily not telling the other maid that I knew one of them. I wished you had been here so I could have told you the things they said. I could not believe the way he talked about me. It was all I could do not to get sick when I heard the names he called me. His friend seemed to lap it all up, him and his white shoes. What I minded most was that he took the air from me. I could feel him take it from me. Air, like water and light, has its own space and should not be stolen. But I would not beg for mercy after the words had wounded me, it's not good to beg for mercy, because if you have to do that, they won't give it to you. When I'm an old woman I will have learned a lot, as much as I've wanted, but will there be anyone to listen? Maybe I won't care. I hushed the other maid so I could hear more, maybe I shouldn't have. I raged to myself, I didn't want to let her know it was me they were talking about. But you know you have to get over boys like that so I thought I would get them some day, maybe not yet, but some day. I would bide my time like an owl waiting for the night. And when theirs came I would watch them eating their words as if they were sand, trying to spit them and I would not help them, maybe pass them a bit of water, but not much. They were blocking my light with gibberish and they would eventually have to pay. I had to run then, pass them unnoticed, to get up to the corner so he'd think I was waiting for him …

Ruth looked up. 'I'm afraid that's as far as I've got with the letter – I'm having to decipher the faded writing – but I will have more done by our next conference.'

Rosa Maria gurgled with laughter in the back row. The applause that came had a spring in it. Ruth sat down, and the wing of the dead writer breathed past her again. A few people came up to speak to her, including one of those fellows who had been looking over her shoulder at the first talk this morning. He lost himself amongst the others as he sidled up to the desk. Interesting. Ruth saw him leave with the paper in his hand. She smiled. He went straight to TD, who wasn't looking very happy.

'You owe me,' Lachey muttered, as he passed over the paper.

TD glanced at it. That would do. Do lovely, no one would ever know.

The final session began with a ring of heartiness about it. The participants wound up the learning, some with joy, some with the gusto of truth, all dedicated to the teaching of literature as a way to understand science, commerce, politics, war and love.

TD stood to do the wind-up, opened his own notes, did the necessary thanks, and then with a flourish picked up the last page with confident fingers and a knowing smile. He said, 'It is, of course, my privilege to have the last word here and I'm delighted to do so,' and then he consulted the page in his hand. 'Today I went into a haze of confusion with my friend, a kind of quick fog fell over us, kept us hidden from the rest of you as we had our brief skirmish with morality.' What the fuck was this, TD silently moaned, but he couldn't seem to stop himself. 'You will know what happened next. I'm a dab hand at getting the deal while putting distance between me and the ooze of corruption, so I came out of the fog looking as clean as a whistle. In the gullet of the street no one would have known what I am really like.' TD frowned, the silence from the room grew louder, sweat went down the small of his back. He was at the last sentence. It read, 'You do know that stealing words is the same as stealing money, only worse. Remember this is not over yet.' He swallowed hard, people looked at each other, Lachey grinned widely. Who could tell whether he knew what was on the stolen page or not. People began to snigger; Toby pulled himself together, 'Of course all of this is metaphor.' He turned, gulped the glass of water and left the podium. A puzzled, unrhythmic applause happened.

All the walking and the sadness and the seediness brought Lenehan back to the Rutland Square Refreshment Bar, where he had a plate of peas with pepper and vinegar and a ginger beer. Here's where he almost had a change of heart. Here's where the falling silence of those around him made him just a bit uneasy, but who were they to think of him like that. No, he would be fine. He would begin his walk again. He would catch up with them and see how things had turned out.

Ruth stood up and flung her light silk scarf around her neck. She would go to the pub with Rosa Maria and others. She would sip the light of today, while in the far corner of a different place Toby would try to drink some darkness from the night.

Two men walked down the street, they had money between them. They faded into significance as if they were stepping on to the page of a book.

The Lie of the Land

Confusion was the first thing that Hugh felt when he was told that his driver was downstairs with an urgent message. He was sure that he had left him at home with his wife, his job for the day to take her around fine-tuning the finishing touches to the charity ball. So how could he be here? There were certainly no visits to be done in this area. And none of their friends lived around here, so his wife certainly couldn't be calling on anyone to flash around lists. It was a delaying tactic, this confusion, giving him time to wonder who was dead. Recently, he had begun to do that, every time an unexpected call came into his office. Odd thing to be doing, continuously wondering who was dead.

He took the lift downstairs, smoothing the blue shirt that was shining with newness – he never let shirts age here, why would he, they were so cheap. Hugh straightened his back, preparing himself for the savage heat and the torpor that would engulf him if he had to step outside the front door, that is if his driver had had difficulty parking and was not in the lobby. The doors swished open with a wet sound. It went with the hush of the tumbling waterfall and the faint sound of the gamelan that was coming through the speaker system. And there was Rhami. In the lobby. He looked as if someone was dead.

And the next thing that came to Hugh, as the now irritating confusion lifted, was a word. Is this what 'denouement' means? Is this what all these years of wandering have come to, all that moving from one country to the other, starting a new life every few years as if the next one could be better? Is this the inevitable result – stepping towards a man who should have been a stranger, impatience mixing with a speeding heartbeat, waiting to hear who was dead?

Rhami told him that he had news from the master's home, not good news. Spit it out, Hugh thought. Who?

'I am afraid that your father had died,' Rhami said, slowly, mixing his tenses as usual.

And I won't even be able to go to the funeral, thought Hugh. Yes, perhaps that is what could be called a denouement. He rubbed his hands together, and felt the heat of them, even in the air-conditioned lobby. His hands were always hot, a medical condition, not related to the amount of alcohol continuously in his system.

'I am sorry, sir,' said Rhami.

Why hadn't Dervla come herself? Why had she sent their driver? Could she not bear to see him think his thought?

'Madam is in the car.'

At least that was something.

Hugh moved outside the foyer of his office block, saw the car parked a mere few yards away. He ran to it. Dervla got out and stared at him. She seemed puzzled, at a loss for words. She did put her arms around him.

'Will you come home now?' she said then.

And Hugh didn't know if she meant to their rich barricaded house or to their youth.

'We'll see,' he said, and they both got into the back of the car.

'Will I drive, sir?' Rhami asked, unnecessarily.

'Yes, do that,' Hugh said, closing the door, forgetting to tell his secretary that he was leaving, forgetting to get his jacket.

They drew out into the miles of backed-up traffic, Rhami beeping and seeping his way into a spot. Unusually, Hugh did not look at how he did this. Unusually, Dervla did. The two of them tacitly agreed to use Rhami's presence as a brake on speaking freely, which was odd, considering the other things he had seen and heard over the two years of his employment with them. Dervla did not notice the stalls, the busy dressmaking shops tacked on to the front of the shanties, the bursting orange of the flower racks. Although she did not always see everything now – outsiders becoming insiders faster than she would have thought possible – she did usually see the flowers. She believed that you could see them grow in the choking heat, even though they were already in buckets of water. As they passed the statue of the fleeing horses, both Hugh and she made themselves ready for getting into the house.

Rhami beeped the horn and the boy opened the wooden double doors and closed them, after the car had sidled in. They stepped out of the jeep and quickly into the cool of the house, still quiet. It was at moments like these that Dervla hated having a maid, and a cook and a cleaner. They had more English than you'd imagine, making free conversation difficult. She walked on the warm tiles to the side of the pool. The staff never went near that, except to clean it. Hugh would follow her. She looked up at the iron

25

railings around their garden, sat down and put her feet in the water, to ease a mosquito bite between her toes. The green was burned out of the grass, leaving it a silvery grey. Particles of faded brown clay lay half-heartedly exposed. Truly, even the earth was tired of the heat.

Hugh stood at the wall-sized window and looked down to the end of the garden at Dervla's back. Her shadow sat beside her, perfectly formed and totally black, there being no cloud in the sky. He could smell the chlorine waving in and out of the heat fumes.

It was Hugh who had got them into this predicament. One quick, minute lie, a fib of a thing really, in his opinion. A small deception that had rolled over their lives, like an iceberg, pulling chunks out of them, and discarding them at will, depositing them like human drumlins in all sorts of places.

Dervla and he had had jobs in the national television station, Raidió Teilifís Éireann, jobs that others thought were bursting at the seams with possibility. The year was 1980, and the decade was shaping up to have its share of excitements. But they were both unhappy at their work, constrained, and taken aback by the frequency of pension talk. They were twenty-two years old. It was this guilty dissatisfaction that drew them conspiratorially closer. Over canteen tea and glasses of Harp in Madigan's, they talked of faraway places. It was he who had fallen in love with the idea of South Africa; it was she who had said that they couldn't go there because of the politics, the boycott.

'And no one would ever speak to us again,' she said.

'I'm not political,' he said.

'But I don't think it's about *you* being political,' Dervla replied.

Ah well.

Afterwards she knew that she should have been more definite. More confident in her argument. Indeed, put up a proper argument. So, she had to take a share of the blame. In no time at all, Hugh had jobs secured for them in Cape Town. How he had done this was still a mystery to Dervla, the secrecy of it adding to the charm, she had to admit; the secrecy now doing driving of its own. Marriage was the way to cement it, and would make travelling easier too.

'Perth. You're going to Perth,' Dervla's colleague said to her. 'We didn't know you were thinking of leaving at all. Hugh just told us.'

'Perth,' Dervla squeaked, blushing furiously.

She sidled over to Hugh's desk. He muttered, 'Not now – meet me outside in fifteen minutes.'

At the door she croaked, 'What were you thinking?'

'Look, it just slipped out,' he pleaded.

'I couldn't stand the thought of them looking at me, you know the embargo and that, so it slipped out. It will be okay, honestly it will.'

Dervla wasn't sure. The lie made her extra nervous, and things were bad enough as it was. 'Maybe we could go there, to Perth, you know?'

'No, it's too late. We'd lose all our money.'

He looked so distraught that Dervla placated him. 'It's none of their business anyway where we go,' she said, doubtfully.

Well, if it wasn't, they made it. They talked non-stop about kangaroos. In the second week some of them had graduated to possums and boomerangs. A subtle competition had begun at the desks around Dervla. Who could come up with the most unlikely thing to say about Australia. And say it as if they'd known it all along.

'I suppose you'll become an opera buff?'

'That's Sydney I think.'

'*Ór, airgead, copar, luaidhe, stán, gual agus iarann,*' said the boss, showing not only that he remembered the minerals of Australia, but that he had gone to an all-Irish school – two things for the effort of one. Dervla thought that her notice would never be worked. The worst was the last-night party. First, they both had to ensure that none of their families turned up, dropping hints about their own credentials on the apartheid issue. And then they had to wear bush hats all night. Hugh's boss's wife had made them herself. The corks hit into Dervla's eyes every time she moved. And then they had to get guarantees that no one from work would turn up at the airport.

'Hugh's mother,' Dervla murmured. 'She'd be too upset to deal with people she doesn't know.'

'Of course,' they said.

As for their families and the airport – most of them cried off at the last minute, the political objections being just too strong to overcome, and those that did turn up managed to have parked awkwardly and needed to get back to their cars quickly. At Heathrow they relaxed.

'No one here gives a fiddler's which long-distance flight we're getting. Isn't it great?' Hugh said. Dervla still wasn't sure. Checking departure times, it was impossible not to see the Australian flights, no matter how fast they tried to gallop their eyes past them.

The first month was fresh and a little frightening. 'But we'll get used to it,' Hugh said. And then a word entered their lives. Stole into every day to mock them. Irony.

They did not like South Africa. Hugh in particular.

He thought about the word all the time. It was meant to have a funny component to it. This had none. And soon news came of Hugh's brother meeting the man who had sat at the desk next to Dervla.

'So how do they like Perth?'

'Perth, is it!' he guffawed. 'Let me tell you ...'

It would be all over the office now, buzzing with a life of its own, flying with impunity from one side of the open plan to the other, stopping en route to pick up embellishment, like a bee would stick pollen to its rear end. Both of the mothers told them this story as kindly as they could. They still kept in touch, as mothers will. But they were almost the only ones. Distance grew in peculiar geometric shapes. Dervla knew that she was now a lying stranger to every single friend she'd ever known. She tried not to think about it. Hugh rushed to pick the next place they could go to live. The organisation of it would take his mind off things. And if that one didn't work out, they could try another. And another. And they did.

And that is how they came to be living here, a few degrees from the equator.

In the mornings the men went out to get more oil. The women maybe played mahjong. Some of them, bored with being bored, counted down to gin time; some avoided this by building a charity circle. Dervla did that. All that endless possibility was now wound tight in these charity evenings. If she stopped, there was a danger that she could hit a wall with the recoil. The women piled together on these nights and grew extraordinary tolerance towards unexpected behaviour – one could never tell what a person was thinking, what news had come that day. Dervla tried to avoid tidings from Ireland, they upset her like songs. But she loved titbits from England, or better still, Scotland. Some Welsh stories had zest, although their dinner dances never took off, never quite lodged themselves into the night. People left them early. Dervla couldn't figure out why.

A cousin of Hugh's had visited one time, to date their only guest. He brought lots of news and Dervla took in the bits she wanted to hear. They brought him to a dance and introduced him to all sorts. He said he couldn't see the point; it wasn't as if he'd be back again. Dervla loved the sound of him, and brought him to all the places that she thought might interest him. He was most taken by the hundreds of men making a human chain to unload the boats.

'Or see those ones, scuttling like ants. We don't know what work is.'

'True,' Dervla said, while thinking that a body can never tell what will impress another.

But although she loved the sound of him, by the end of the week she felt drained by the effort of translating her life to him. He didn't seem to have replies to most of what she said.

It became hard to remember not knowing this place, to imagine their first month. It had been Hugh who had chosen it.

'This will be the best place,' he had said, with made-up confidence.

Dervla had been appalled by the heat. She thought that it might actually melt her. It seemed predatory, following her everywhere, even into dark corners. But she forced herself out, visiting the women who called in the first week. There was no question of her getting a job. She learned the manners from the women. Do not shout at your staff. (You can say what you like behind their backs.) Do not stand with your hands on your hips. Do not touch a child on the head. So strange that one, when touching a child on the head should be such a laying on of love and luck. Some of what they told her might have fallen short on accuracy, but Dervla had no choice but to believe.

The conversation of the women wove an artificial normality. The endless comparisons between this minute and back home were not as tiresome as they might have been, acting as touchstone rather than boast. They could talk well, these women; they were widely lived abroad and depended totally on each other's idleness to make a country for themselves. And if, in the beginning, Dervla thought one woman disconcertingly like the next, she soon learned how to match story to name.

At Christmas they decamped, the men too, to a hotel by the beach. Being out of the city made them into quieter people, and the luxury of their surroundings released their strains dangerously fast. In the languid calm of early morning, Dervla heard birds singing. What a sound. She wasn't sure if there were any birds in their city, singing away there behind the noise. She slipped out of bed and made her way silently to the water's edge. The doorman put his hands together and bowed to her. The graciousness of it made the backs of her eyes wince. Three fishing boats were already rocking on their outriggers a half-mile out to sea. A man swept the beach with a bunch of twigs, scratching the sand with a perfect rhythm into a carpet of hot gold. Dervla, in her sarong, walked through the edges of the already warm water. On the Atlantic coast in winter, you could be mesmerised into the torrential sea, called by the wild, definitely by the unreasonable, otherwise why would you wade in, up to your knees, freezing your legs that would then tickle with cold for hours. Dervla felt a little like crying. She called into the temple on her way back.

'Are you menstruating?' the guide asked, as he wrapped the cloth around her.

'No,' she said.

She would not have lied.

That night eight of them shared a table. The massages had been had during the day, toenails had been painted, the sea had been properly entered. The wine was hearty. Dervla sat opposite Hugh. Beside him was Louise, the best talker of all the women. Her stories came fully formed. Tonight she was talking of the house of fakers.

'No. 45, on your street.'

'Tell them why you call it that, go on.'

She explained that the wife had drunkenly told her one night that her husband was the man who had faked a series of historical diaries, made a fortune, but, just as they were beginning to learn how to spend the money, he was found out. They were now in shamefaced hiding and would have to remain here forever, never to hear their own language liquidly spoken again.

'Funny, a man at home forged a Famine diary, but somehow he survived,' Hugh said. 'Yes, odd that. He now looks like a banker. Maybe not now, it's a long time since I've seen him,' he added, more or less to himself.

And talk was spun of other fakers. The Ukrainian, recently arrived in Australia, who had won the literary prize for the truth and authenticity that the growing up in the Ukraine had given her voice. She was from Bath, but had flown over Kiev once, on her way to Brisbane.

'Or so she thought, but how could you know for sure? Flying over Kiev, I mean.'

And the footballer who had pretended to have cancer and wept when he thanked the locals who had collected a fortune to fund the best possible treatment for him. There had been pictures of him crying in all the newspapers. And the woman who had pretended to have children. She had forgotten their names, on a night like this, so she too was found out. And women who pretended to be men so they

32

could be sailors, fight wars and play in jazz bands. And men who pretended to be women just so they could be women. They laughed at that. All the ripples of laughter were in agreement. Hugh was happy. This place had worked out the best of them all.

'That's us,' said Dervla.

'What?'

'That's us. Fakers. Liars.'

'What do you mean us?' Louise asked sharply, always a little tetchy about the oil money.

'Not all of us, or at least I don't know. But us, Hugh and me.'

'And I.'

They turned their faces to her. Someone coughed another question. But Dervla had nothing more to say, and lowered her eyes in the direction of her plate. They turned their faces to Hugh. They allowed a little silence and then prodded him to deny such a thing. But Hugh looked into his glass. She would never forgive him, he thought. God, no, she would never ever forgive him.

Hugh couldn't remember how the evening had been publicly rescued. But it had. And he and Dervla had walked hand in hand up the magic pathway to their bedroom. The others had staggered their leave-taking, trying to be nonchalant about it, trying to pretend that they had not longed for Hugh and Dervla to go first. There was no need for that – couldn't they ring each other from their rooms later. When Hugh closed the door, a degree of intimacy that he and Dervla had managed to preserve, despite everything, was locked out with the turn of the key.

Yes, higher intimacy left them that evening. And although they both did their best to bury Dervla's lapse, her voice became melancholy, and Hugh's occasional

33

impatience became louder and more pronounced. Heaven knows it wasn't as if he couldn't get more cheerful, more grateful company in this place. But he never had. No, he never had. And he congratulated himself on that, as if fidelity had made a hero of him. In the late evenings Dervla became particularly distant, and if she woke in the middle of the night she got up and wandered about. He could hear her padding around sometimes.

And now here they were, she waiting for him to join her at the pool, her back with its shadow turned away from him. And when he did, and put his own feet in the pool, she put out her hand and squeezed his. They sat for a few moments, trying to make up a silence from out of the endless noise. Oil boys, who came a few times a day to check on the safety of employees, could be heard rapping on selected doors. The echo followed the boys to the end of the streets.

'I suppose he'll be buried in Calvary Chapel,' Dervla said, rubbing the back of Hugh's hand.

'I suppose. Where else.'

Hugh had made his mind up. But he would not tell her yet. He would let it emerge. One thing was for sure, he was not going to go back, to be pointed at. Even though he could bet that all sorts of people were now slipping into their conversations the fact that they had been to South Africa years ago. In secret. They could slide that in quickly, now that the whole thing was sorted. But no, he was not going to stand tormented by every gap that happened in conversation, wondering what it meant.

They went inside and nibbled at food. They could reach no agreed conclusion and by late evening their occasionally raised voices ebbed out with exhaustion. They gave up and went to bed, where Dervla comforted Hugh

In the morning, she woke to the sound of a rooster crowing against the call to prayer. Cock of the dung heap. King of all he surveys. At home. The cars had already started blowing their horns and, if she had looked outside, Dervla could have seen small, uniformed, sleepy children on their way to school. She tiptoed into the spare bedroom, the room that mocked their lack of visitors. She took down the case and started putting things into it. She put another on the floor beside it. Maybe. She would take that top and those skirts. And that jewellery box. She loved packing. It was the only time that she could see, properly, the bits and pieces that she had accumulated in all their wanderings. The case was in the hallway when Hugh got up for breakfast.

'You'll need Rhami to bring you to the airport,' he said, as they sipped their tea. And he didn't even look at her.

'Okay,' she said, afraid of the certainty in his voice.

'And I'll see you,' Hugh said, 'when …'

'Okay,' she said. And got up from the table, wiped her hands on the towel that was hanging on the cupboard door and went to get her case, while Hugh called out for Rhami.

Dear You

Dear You,

And yes, you're right, it is the old letter in the bottle. I do apologise for the melodrama of it. We have all heard about such a thing but truly do not expect to be a recipient. And of course, I know not if this will ever be read. Still, I write as if it will. And if you are perusing it may I welcome you to my story. Do leave it until you have got home if it is a cold day or until you are sitting on a bench if it is warm, with invigorating air, oh how I remember straightening air like that on sea walks. In Dublin in particular, on a Sunday. I think perhaps a bottle has a better chance of washing up in the tossed aftermath of a storm. Although, mind you, flotsam and jetsam can arrive on calm days too. I think this missive is a bit of both of those things; a small part of the wreckage of my life and a small part of goods thrown overboard to lighten the mind in distress. But I should also say that not all of my life is shaded in gloom. I have days in which order and intent and garden walks lend me certain calmness, even cheerfulness.

If you are reading this letter it means that George really did do as I asked. He promised he would, but I've been on the receiving end of those kind of assurances before. I discovered last month that all the letters I have given Matron to post have been piled up in a corner, not one of them sent. It was a terrible blow, one final kick. Over all these years. Hard to believe. All the letters putting forward the reasons why I should now be released, all the letters asking to be moved to a convent so that I could serve my days there, all the letters explaining the process of my thoughts and my actions, every one of them piled on top of each other gathering dust. Strange that they kept them; you would think that they could at least have burned them – that might have accorded them their seriousness. But no, just piled up in a corner getting old and unread. So, you see, I have no choice but to try this other way. And it will be my last attempt, I know when I'm beaten.

Yes, my last attempt, unless of course you find this during my lifetime and come to visit me, which is a little unlikely I think. This letter may seem an overly theatrical gesture on my part, and it may not indeed have turned out to be necessary, because perhaps by the time you've got this, my name, and those of the others, are already well known and my action and theirs truly appreciated. Oh, I have just thought, maybe there are more than one of you reading this, two or three of you even, taking an early morning stroll in England, or imagine perhaps in Ireland, ah Ireland, or France, where I was a free woman, or Italy even. Maybe even in Italy. Wouldn't that be just perfect.

Because of the possible pointlessness of sending this, I am leaving a lot to your imagination, an intimate sort of thing to do to a stranger, but I hope you will understand.

Let me get to the point. I am penning this to you, via the gardener, from the asylum in Northampton, where I have been forcibly lodged now for the last thirty years. It's the early 1950s and I've been here since 1927. They call me the Irish woman who shot Mussolini, because that is what I am. They still say that I am insane to have done such a thing, even though they sent thousands upon thousands upon thousands to their deaths to do that very deed. It is a burden to carry, to have done the right thing early. But one that I accept with as good grace as I can, not all the time of course, I have my days of rage, but mostly I try to live my life with as much manners as I can muster and with my eye on the birds and the flowers and the grass outside. So far, I have always had a window in my room and a bigger one nearby. And when I'm out walking in the garden I sometimes talk to George, and when he said that he and his wife were going to Folkestone I thought to pen this letter. You see it seems right to put something of me in Folkestone, something to go with my last free steps. Even if the note had not made it to you it would still be something of me, thrown in the water there, because I was happy the last time I looked down at the moody waves gliding under our boat. And it seemed a good spot too because a bottle could go places from there.

I will begin near the beginning, although it is hard to know what bits of our beginning make us take action, or not, as is the case with most people; what bits make us be part of the wider world looking out, often the same things that make a sibling gather into themselves and step back into the comfort of their own pettiness.

My family and I lived at Number 22 Merrion Square in Dublin. It was a grand house, still is I expect – it had an alcove for the white Carrara marble statue of Paolo and

Francesca da Rimini that my father had bought at a Milan art exhibition two years before he was made Attorney General of Ireland, which was two years before I was born, the seventh child with one more to come. Our ceilings were by Adam and we had Bartolozzi engravings, certainly enough beauty to make our lives easy. I don't remember much about my childhood; it would appear that I stamped my feet a lot, but then families do tell tales like that when they want to get an answer to something they do not understand. They think that if they can bring the adult down to their early size, they will be able to belittle the action, oh yes, I've seen it. I've heard it. Over and over again. And they think they win. Well let them. Sorry, I shouldn't be involving you in this, indeed I shouldn't be involving myself in it, it's a counterproductive reductionism that does nothing for the intellectual facts of my actions. So, I will leave it, for the moment anyway, and will try to stop myself if I stray into it again, a difficult thing to do in this place when I remember where I am, dropped into Northampton, which means nothing to me at all, even though there have been poets here before me and you would think that could give it something to cling to.

When I was nine years old my father was made Lord Chancellor of Ireland. I remember all the talk about it. I remember the flurrying of carriages, the endless sounds of horses pulling up outside, even at night. I think the boys in the house got more important then, and the girls were expected to do even less than we had done before, but with a lot of dressing up. I didn't attach undeserved seriousness to that but I went along with it, not knowing what else to do. We had school at home. I particularly liked languages, which were really being taught to my brothers so they could fight wars, if necessary, even where English was not spoken. My French is still good, all our time at Boulogne-sur-Mer polished it nicely, and my Italian is a particular love. The Italians still have the best poems. We read what we were told to read until I discovered that you could find other books too, some of which I got from Willie. I should tell you that of my seven siblings – Willie, Harry, Elsie, Edward, Victor, Frances and Constance – only three really matter to me, which is not too bad really. Two of the three who matter to me are now dead.

I did my best to mostly fit in, despite my reading. I occasionally brought up a conversation about women voting – I read of it sometimes – and my father congratulated himself that he approved. But I knew that he would want to tell us how to do it if it ever did happen. He had a way of looking at me, rather startled, when I mentioned it. The same look he used when he said, Enough is Enough. I could hear the capitals on the words. And when that day did come, years after he died, I remember that I asked my sister not to put on a corset just for once. I said to her, 'For heaven's sake, we're going to vote,' and she looked at me like our father used to do.

Before the voting day, well before that, I had been presented as a debutante at the court of Queen Victoria. And that is one of the things I should remember but can't quite recall, maybe a sound of rustling dresses comes to me, but perhaps I don't recall it because I don't want to. I see it as belonging to a time before I had learned of the hunger that had lapped at the corner of our elegant street, had realised some of the unjust workings of our world and had become interested in theosophy, which allowed for no flippant discrimination. My father gave me money of my own when I was twenty-one, and no, I didn't earn it, but it allowed me to examine how to live a useful life.

When I was twenty-six, I became a Catholic. It seemed the right, the most engaged thing to do. The announcement of my conversion in the newspaper put an end to notice of any of the more trivial aspects of my life. The family row was all enveloping, how much time it took. What a silly thing for people to get into such a state about how others live their lives. Maybe it is a thing to be envied, to have such energy for interference in what is not one's own existence.

It was then that I went to London, left the bickerings behind me. I knew the city well, had been to parties and knew too that there was a different life to be had there, that I could escape from the tornado of spite visited upon me by most members of my family and by my acquaintances.

Let me speak a little to you of my family. I do not believe that blood relation is important simply because of plasma and, if it is necessary to do so, escaping it can be the hardest but most important feat of one's life. On the other hand, we can have one or more relative who affects us to the good, or one or more whom we love as we might a friend. But often we have some whose every reaction we know intimately, while trying to forget them and hating what they are doing to the freedoms of our mind. There are siblings who would choke every thought you have – throttlers of imagination. They are the ones who resent the grammar of all foreign language.

Of my brothers I have this to say: I loved Harry, the tobogganer. I loved the sport of him, the long look of him. And wouldn't it be he who got tuberculosis and died. I can feel the fondness that I had for Victor – he died young too. Edward was all right I must suppose. But it was Willie I loved best. He gave me books, he took me around London, he accepted my mind, we talked of all things, modernism among them, and how that fitted our lives. My two sisters Elsie and Frances married well, that's all I have to say about them. Constance was all that her name meant. And, although she is the person who allowed me to go through France a free woman for the last time and did not tell me, she is also the one who visited me and perhaps did her best. Perhaps. Perhaps. Willie, who knew what new thoughts were to go with the old, who dreamed with me, who knew me, who made me laugh too, did not turn up in Paris when our train went through, did not turn up and take me off. I try to find excuses for him, reasons that might have stopped him coming. Perhaps he was too removed by then. When my father died, we saw that he had sat and written the words that cut Willie out of his will, a nasty unforgiving thing to do. The sentence had a vicious sheen all of its own. He did not cut me out to the same extent, because he would have thought that my difference could not be so dangerous, me being female. Well, there.

Once settled in London, I did indeed make myself useful with the poor, it was the least I could do. I also had a life that comes with the beginning of a century, when the darkness of the last can be put away. I kept track of what that light was doing in Dublin. Willie had been a Catholic now for a long time. He believed in the right of Ireland to run its own affairs, he spoke and dreamed in Irish. He always had news of Dublin. But then he veered his life towards Compiègne, hardly the most engaged thing to be doing. I saw him as much as I could, between the comings and goings. Have I told you that he was my favourite? Constance was learning to behave like an unmarried daughter.

In Chelsea I learned about freedom and about love. That's what it was. It is a time that I don't like to think about, comparison will make me weak with longing. I will lose my voice. When you have learned those two things, freedom and love, you see things in a different way. The constraints that your family have tried to put on you become clear for what they are, frantic fears they will not be able to control what you think or read or how you see the world and what colours you decide to see it through. It was a lovely time there, keeping up with news of suffrage things. And art. And talk of those Pankhursts. They had nerve. I admired that and always remembered what it took. After all the living in Chelsea I learned to feel the distance appropriate to a grown-up.

When my fiancé died, I slept among his clothes, inhaling him up so he would be inside me. It helped, or so I thought, although it is difficult to remember just how black my days became, one long tunnel of hours soaked with grief. It wrapped itself around me, made its way into my pores and finally struck me ill. People had to move back a few inches from the aura of my sadness, otherwise its strength would have hurt them. But I got well enough to go to my father's funeral in Dublin – I had read of his death in the evening edition of the newspaper. It's hard to know if it's worth making these gestures, certainly most of the rest of them didn't think so. Perhaps they were right.

I believe that my response to this isolation, to remove to Paris and work for a pacifist organisation, was the correct one. It seems such a little thing to have done now, after what happened. But it didn't seem so then, it appeared that we might be able to stop the plunge into war. We believed that, before the future. And who is to say that it was wrong of us to hope. And when we couldn't be heard above the din of battle cries I went back to London, knowing the crossing well by now.

We did our best during that first awful carnage. I heard about Ireland, the small nation, making its attempt. I heard about the executions and wondered what Dublin felt. I missed it then. I got ill again and well again and ill again, I'm not sure how many times, before I finally set out for Rome in 1924, to watch a new tyrant growing. I had read about and followed carefully his insidious gathering of control. I went to stop him. It seemed a wise thing to do. And it was.

In Rome I lived a good life. I walked the streets, breathed the air around the endless history of its buildings, tended to the poor as was my wont, prayed in chapels that took the breath from the prayers with their beauty. My mind flickered and shone with lit candles. I read and learned. I had my favourite places, Nero's house was one. I loved looking across to the ruins, imagining the chariots racing before the crowds. I did have a brief illness, when the sadness overcame me, but these things can happen, and it is possible to step back into measured days again. There's a flow to life you know. My nurse, Mary McGrath, and I repaired to a quiet convent on Via delle Isole, one that took in travellers like us. I can still feel it, the solitude, the glorious singing of nuns, the birds flitting from one lemon tree to the other.

It's funny what you actually remember, the things that appear not to be important, but they have a smell about them that makes them different and thus they stay. They matter. I remember that the convent had dark corners, good for hiding in when the sun was too hot. And I remember the smell of the linoleum polish. I've smelled none as sweet since. I and Mary McGrath found refuge there. That comfort sometimes comes to me vividly, fleetingly, when I waken in this asylum. Or when I imagine I hear a nun softly running up and down the gamut before bursting into a hymn. But enough of that, you must be wondering how I got from there to here and I will do my best to explain.

Despite the beauty of Rome, despite its paintings, its pencil-thin trees rising inexplicably towards the blue skies, its lavish avenues and its bright sunsets, there was a rotting thing growing through that man Mussolini and his followers. He was destroying Italy, leading it into the fold of his own ego. We could see it, those of us who spread out the map to its full size. As the deeds of this emerging tyrant and his followers grew in darkness and violence I decided upon action. I was old enough by then to know that sometimes there is nothing else, that action is the only sane choice. I got myself ready and set forth to put my destiny and Mussolini's within a breath of each other.

I remember clearly the morning of my deed. I got up at 6 a.m. and went to Mass, had breakfast and tidied my room, not expecting to be back in it. I thought the tidying was the least I could do. I told the nuns that I would return for lunch, it seemed only fair to pretend for a little while. But I knew that no matter what happened I would never see that bed again. I packed carefully. I wrapped my Lebel revolver in my black veil. I had twenty bullets hidden in my room, I would not require all of them. I put a good-sized stone in the pocket of my dress in case I needed it for breaking the car window. I closed the gate of the convent quietly so as not to disturb the prayers that had already started to create the day. I walked past the lovely doors of Via delle Isole, past the gates opening on to secret gardens, dripping with flowers and slippy green leaves. I could have turned back but I left behind those quiet places and came out on to the thoroughfare.

The streets were busy with lots of visitors for Easter. I watched people linked together as they walked and talked.

I have never resented that; I had it once and although I will never have it again, I do not unreasonably envy those who can slip their hands around the cloth of another's arm without thinking of their privilege. It was an April day, the sky full of sun, anything could be possible on a day like that, and it almost was. I could have succeeded in shooting Mussolini, I was within inches of it. Clearly, I aimed correctly, like my brother had taught me in the hallway in Merrion Square. I did indeed make a mark on him. But in the end my gun let me down and the force of the crowd stymied my next attempt.

On my way through the streets and piazzas I was not, of course, thinking of failure. I was thinking about how I had finally resolved the question of whether it is ever right to kill. I was satisfied that it was and that this tyrant, who still had the world fooled, needed to be stopped in his dark tracks. I passed through the Porta Pia, feeling the stone in my pocket. Although my intentions were to shoot him when he came outside, one could never be absolutely sure of his movements. After all, a man who has butchered and tortured thousands already, a man who has had thirty million photographs of himself in varying athletic poses issued to the world, a man who thinks the people blessed to look into his eyes, that sort of man intends to prance about for as long as possible. Such a man will not be careless about himself and, although he may pretend to be brave, he will indeed change his arrangements continuously in order to stay alive. You know they say that many women wanted to have tea with him, but there were many more who were on my side, of that I am sure, because I felt them that day, a surge of fear-banishing strength, such a wonderful thing.

I had left behind me the Convent of Santa Brigida – so apt that it was our Irish saint's name – left Via delle

46

Isole, gone down Via Nomentana, all the time feeling the stone but not drawing attention to myself. I was thinking of normal things, not too nervous, when I got caught in a moving crowd that was surging to catch a glimpse of something. Ah, so he was here among the splendour of Campidoglio. According to my research he was to speak at the Palazzo del Littorio that afternoon, that's where I was heading, but here he was now. I should take the chance that was given to me. Perhaps I could get him at this moment. I elbowed my way closer and closer, right beside one of the pillars. For once in that spot, I was not noticing the beauty around me. I was focused only on getting as close as I could. A group of students were singing that stupid song that went with the photographs – you will always get some young people who are, frighteningly, already clambering up the landscape of approval. Mussolini turned to them, to soak up more adoration, and it was at that moment I felt the surge of strength. That's what it was. Then it was easy.

My first shot drew a great amount of blood and caused a gasp of silence, like a deep breath being suddenly taken in. I saw the blood pouring down his face and thought I had done it, but then realised he hadn't fallen, so I would need another attempt. I shot again but I'm afraid to say my gun did not perform, the bullet got stuck. I did not succeed. I heard the crowd getting its voice back and then they launched themselves at my body, kicking me, pulling my hair, stamping on me, pulling my collar to bits. I could not get my gun to point again. The crowd pummelled me, their anger ferocious. I watched it as if it was far away. They were going to kill me, but the police shouted that I was theirs and dragged me into the courtyard of the Museo dei Conservatori. I lay on the ground, hearing the melee outside, the shouting coming from the square as Mussolini was carried away. It was a tremendous thing, that noise that I had caused. I opened my eyes and saw the colossal foot of the statue of Constantine. A cat lay sleeping on it, sunning itself with no thought of me or men. I thought, what a lucky cat.

The police dragged me into a sitting position and started asking me a lot of questions, which was only natural. They kept me there for a while. Time seemed odd to me then. I have no idea how long we stayed there, surrounded by those stone sculptures, from which I drew strength. Occasionally a policeman reported back on the state of the crowd outside. Eventually the people were cleared and it was deemed safe for us to remove to Mantellate prison. I was bundled into a car. I tried to fix my collar but I noticed that it was torn. We crossed over the river but I couldn't see by which bridge. It could have been the Palatino or the Garibaldi. I would still like to know, even though it's not the sort of thing that I would be talking about here. The heavy doors swung open, I remember hearing the flapping of birds' wings as they did, a huge soar of them went towards the sky. And I heard a bell ringing nearby, perhaps the Mantellate bell itself. The doors closed. For all I know the birds soared again.

Someone took my fingerprints and then moved me towards the nun-jailers. I thought of other things as they strip-searched me, it is possible to do that if you have learned to pray. I did not like them taking my hairclips. My holy medals had already been torn from my neck by the mob. They did clean my cuts up before they passed me back for more questioning, which was good of them really. I was alive and the blows of the crowd had been attended to. That poor boy, Matteo, that poor young boy, was not afforded the same gestures. He tried to do the same as me, six months later in Bologna. He took aim in another beautiful piazza but this time the crowd made no mistake. They left him dead. I go silent for a while, even now, when I think of him, that brave boy. He deserves a moment's silence. But back to my questioning – they made a shocking fuss of the piece of paper with that morning's directions written on it, Palazzo del Littorio. It's where Mussolini was meant to go. 'So, you intended shooting him?' Of course I intended shooting him. I did not answer them, nor did I tell them where I got the gun. That is still my secret.

I was fifty when I shot Mussolini, a good age I think to do it, don't you? I would really have liked not to have upset everyone, but I couldn't not have done it just to keep my family happy.

I'm not sure why, but I seem to have fallen into trying to explain myself here. While I do think you deserve that, really you either think it was a good idea or you don't. And I do. But you may be having difficulty with the idea of a woman doing it. Mussolini certainly did – they say he exclaimed to himself, What! A woman! He didn't like that.

A move was then put in place to prove that I was mad. And how do you do that? What does mad mean? And if once mad for an hour or two, does that mean forever? Yes, I had already directed harm to myself but then I was not the first thinking human to do that. Look at Emily Davison, she too took the hopeless route, although certainly not on the day of the Derby: she had her return fare paid and a ticket to the suffrage dance that night. (I was so glad that Father was dead before all that, not that I would have had to listen to him by then, but Constance and Mother would.)

In Mantellate jail, with the bell ringing in time with all the other bells, and the river flowing nicely outside, they said that my lack of desire to have children was a sign that I was mad. And how they rushed to do their gynaecological examination. I looked at the ceiling and prayed to any god I could get to come into my head; I kept my eyes wide open so as not to give them the comfort of seeing me close them. One of the jailers got me Professor Gianelli's report. She smuggled it in to me. I have always been able to get on well with staff, yes, it was best to think of my jailers as that. Still is. The fine professor, a snake of a man, wrote to the Prosecutor that he had proceeded to undertake the examination, that the prisoner had submitted to it without protest. That means he noticed that I had kept my eyes open. He went on to say that the hymen was not intact, he said that it permitted with ease the introduction of two exploratory fingers, that's his two fingers. He went on to talk about squeezing my urethra. He would. The hymen is not intact. Indeed. I could have told him that. And made it sound a good and joyful thing.

Perhaps I need to spend some more time on this notion of mad. Yes, I have my moments, short bursts of terrible anger. It is unfortunate that I have not learned to control these now only annual events. But I ask you, I ask you, what is that small rare fizz of mine in comparison to the legal rage of free men who walk the streets and run the armies? Of course, it is not a good plan to lash out, and each time I do it I realise that I am giving them more fodder for their interpretation of me, more sustenance to the notion that I need to be locked up forever. (By the way, I am not sorry that I hit Mrs —. If you had to listen to the monotone of her so would you.) But I digress. It seems to me that rage can be a right thing. We would not have the vote without it, I imagine you saying that is not true, that it would have been granted in time, but I ask you to look at the places in the world, even in the 1950s, that do not have it. Maybe in the future, when you have found this, women not having the vote will be unthinkable anywhere. And maybe not. You understand by now that I was not a woman who spent my life frittering at sewing. I shouldn't demean sewing, it is in fact a thing I would like to be able to do, the in and out of the needle, the strict mechanics of the thing. Perhaps it could remove the mind to higher things, but the perceived docility of it always put me off. If you look around a door and see a room full of women sewing, you do not think of action. And I believed in action. Still do.

You may be wondering how I got from Rome to here. After they had assaulted my inner self, they continued the relentless questioning about an international conspiracy. Surely a woman could not have done this on her own? Surely a woman could not have seen what this festering tyrant was doing? Surely a woman could not have known that tyranny incubates and flies across borders? Mussolini and his men used this constructed conspiracy to further imprison, burn and butcher swathes more of those who understood the danger of him. Meanwhile I stayed in jail while they wondered what to do with me. They allowed faithful Mary McGrath to see me once. They would no doubt have questioned her about our stay in the convent, about where I went, who I saw. I do hope she survived all that. I do hope she got back to Ireland all right. They told me that Willie came. And Constance. They told me that letters I had best not see were written about me. I can only imagine the spite that some would have spewed. They told me that my relatives were not best pleased. They told me that telegrams were sent hoping for the speedy recovery of Mussolini. They told me that in the end he did not want a woman standing trial for shooting him. News that a woman had taken aim, and almost succeeded, could take on a life of its own and lead to his ridicule. So, he had to find a solution. And he and my family and England did.

So, Constance came. And had in her pocket all manner of things to do with my life. And with her came nurses who pretended they were there for my welfare. And a man from Thomas Cook – that still puzzles me. The paperwork complete, our entourage, which also included a goodly number of men, presumably police officers – my, what a fuss – made its way to the railway station.

It was wonderful to smell the morning air at Termini. The pigeons scattered noisily when we went on to the platform. The place smelled of food and work and rush. People shouted at each other with every decibel. There was busyness and parting and meeting. There was colour and laughter. It was bliss for my eyes. We boarded the train around noon, I think. Constance and I had a two-berth sleeper. I could not believe the joy of it. I was almost afraid to accept where I was. The train cranked up its preparation noises and then we were off, whistled out of the station, on our way to my free life. It was a pleasure to watch the suburbs of Rome glide behind our train, on up past Florence. I waved at people now and then and they waved back. Who is to say if they knew me or not? And on through the yellow light flashing into blues, glorious sunshine, fields mirrored in lakes, dazzling silver dancing on bits of the Ligurian Sea, on through all that was beautiful. At the border in Modane, through my half-sleep, I saw Constance exchange papers, the policemen, the nurses and the man from Thomas Cook looking over her shoulder. I closed my eyes. I trusted her. And after the fading of the Italian beauty, a new one, the French, became its own. I had a lovely time on that journey, my heart and head full of harmony.

As the villages of France winked past our train, I felt a great relaxation upon me. I had made a small mistake at the border. I had murmured, as they stood looking at the papers, that I hoped to be back in Italy soon and when they asked me why, I said, to shoot Mussolini, of course. Constance had jumped, a strange frightened jolt, and I had said, oh come Constance, no need to be antsy – it was a word we had used when children and I thought it might have helped her but it was the beginning of her getting more and more nervous while I got calmer and calmer, happy to watch the towns come and shine and fade sedately. If only I had known. If I had known that my life had been signed away but that I was a free woman while whizzing through France, I could have escaped. You may say that would not have been possible, but let me tell you that a woman who came within a quarter of an inch of killing Mussolini could surely have got away from three nurses, a sister and a travel agent. And if I had known I surely could have got Willie to come in from Compiègne when we were passing through Paris, and I could surely have jumped at Boulogne. I knew its streets well enough. But, as I said, I was full of harmony. I bade farewell to the French coast with no fear and I welcomed the coast at Folkestone, saw it as a friend.

Even in Harley Street, as they signed papers, I could not have believed what they had in mind for me. I rather enjoyed the names coming up, Hemel Hempstead, Berkhamsted, all ringing of homestead, Leighton Buzzard, Bletchley, fine names I thought. Even in this asylum, when they put me to bed on my first evening, and brought Constance to the office to explain my life, even then I did not know, could not have guessed, surely could not believe, that my own explanations were never to be heard again. I would never again speak for myself.

Over the years I have found ways of coping, there is not much else I can do. The grounds here give me great solace: the trees are large and I can imagine myself all sorts of places under them. I talk to the birds when needs be. George, the gardener and the postman of this, keeps me up to date with things he thinks might interest me. He told me about Mussolini asking for the gold and of the women who gave up their wedding rings, and of the few who did not and what happened to their children. I did think that when England finally went to war with him, finally saw him for the enemy he was, I did think then that I would be freed. So did George. I was sorry that the bomb dropped on us didn't give me a chance to run. I certainly thought, when they applauded the end of Mussolini's life, that some of that applause would bring good things to me. George thought so too. But it was not to be.

George and I talk about plants a lot. It is what he has in common with me. But he tries to get other things to bring me, I can see him do it. It was him who said that an Irish woman had come, he thought I might know of her or at least of her father, a writer, called James Joyce. I said that I did and I wait to see if we will have much to say to each other, I do hope so. They tell me that she knows France too, and Italy, although not the one I know. Before I speak to her, I should finish this letter.

And so, Dear You, perhaps you are cold by now but I would ask one thing of you. I have made my will stipulating that my funeral should be held in Northampton Cathedral and that I should be buried in the Catholic corner of St Andrew's Cemetery. I have left money for a substantial headstone. Presuming that I am dead by now, could you check for the record if those final wishes have been granted. In conclusion, I am now going to make this into a roll to be put into the bottle that George has promised to throw. He says that he will find the right size, and a good cork, so that the words don't get drowned. I could have said more, perhaps explained more – it may appear to you that I have just given tufts of details – but I hope that it suffices to bring your attention to me and to the others, to let you know that my thoughts and feelings have remained mostly intact, despite the door having been slammed, despite all that was dear to me having been stolen from me, despite the fact that the only way I can speak to you is through this perhaps unreliable bottle.

Signed,
Violet Gibson

Imagine Them

Mary Lee took a look over the big days in her life as she folded her documents carefully. It was hard to believe that such a short glance, such a minor intake and almost unnoticeable holding of breath, could cover all of a lifetime so far. It scanned birth – Mary Walsh, 1821 – marriage and seven givings of birth as if they were any old dates. The bits in between and after weren't on the papers. Nor indeed were they in her head at this precise moment, due to the more immediate concerns that had to be bedded. She tucked her husband's death certificate in the middle; it would be safe there.

'I was born on St Valentine's Day. You know they put him in place of Lupercalia of Fertility.' She thought they might have done that because love seemed a cleaner thing than passion.

Mary had read poetry all her life. It had fitted with the Monaghan hills around her. They folded on top of each other in a vague sort of way, defying absolute definition. Sometimes it was better to be uncertain. When she'd married George, she hadn't minded taking the name Lee, which was a sideways translation for a working poet.

She put the folded papers in an envelope and packed them in the middle of her clothes.

'Maybe you should put them in your bag,' her daughter Evelyn said. 'We'll be able to keep our handbags with us, won't we?'

Evelyn was nineteen years old and hadn't had enough time to imagine how far away Australia was, never mind what a ship journey there would be like.

'They'll be all right here in the trunk – one less thing to have to mind, until we get there.'

They were nearly ready to go, waiting on the horseman. Evelyn walked about so as not to fidget. There was a tone to the day, Mary thought, but that was because her recently dead husband had been an organist, so words like that came to mind easily. Well, she was leaving the music now. And maybe she could depart the livid sorrow too, leave it behind as if it was an animate thing. Maybe the sea would swallow up the ghostly pain that was wracking her small enough frame.

'We're all set then,' she said, as the carriage drew up to take them to the ship.

No one thinks of what it was like for her to close the door. But she had done it before, when leaving Monaghan to go to England, and in its own way that had been every bit as hard and as easy. It had taken a full day to get to Drogheda port for the boat across the Irish Sea. She wasn't sure how long it would take today but thought that their heads would be around their long journey ahead by the time they got to London. Surely.

It was only a week since Mary had told her neighbours that she had decided to go to Australia, Adelaide to be exact. Her son, Ben, who had gone there three years ago, had got ill. It was a good excuse.

'I'll go to mind him, get him better, and Evelyn will come too.'

Not one to like the idea of lying down with the horrors of grief, the thought had come to her very soon after George, her husband, had died. She said the word husband a lot, more often than she'd ever done when he was alive.

'You're thinking of going where?'

They couldn't wait to get home to pass that one about. 'She is not. She couldn't be. Not at her age.'

At the other end of the world, they were waiting for her to match her history with theirs.

That first time, when they got to the Drogheda quay, Bertie Chambers had put their belongings side by side. Mary had stared in wonder; she had never seen a boat before. They stood for some time, listening to horses snorting at the ferocious noise of it all. A boy walked over, checked the name on the trunk, and hoisted it on to his shoulder.

'You can take the rest with you,' he said, looking at the two other bags, which looked small out here in the open.

'Well, I'll leave you to it now. *Go n-éirí an bóthar libh*,' Bertie said with fake heartiness, peering suspiciously at the boat, glad he was turning the horses for home. He looked back once but couldn't make out the shapes of Mary and George.

Along with the other journeyers, Mary and Evelyn had indeed got the gist of travel by the time they got to London.

If Bertie had been there, he would have had some right words.

With one foot on the brand-new *Orient* and one still on land, they suspended belief in time, that would be the best thing to do. And they did manage the journey well enough, give or take a few nights best forgotten. When they put the same foot off the boat in Port Adelaide, only thirty-seven days and twenty-two hours later, they both squinted as if they might see the place better by doing so. They would need new hats for sure to keep this light at bay. They made their way to Ben's house, legs a bit shaky as they felt the thud of their feet on terra firma, the words meaning something only to those who know different.

Mary set to diligent caring but neither that, nor praying, nor hoping, nor her coming this far made her son better. They buried him out under the trees in Walkerville, Mary wrote to the others.

'Will we go home now?' Evelyn asked, not saying what she wanted, simply waiting to hear what was going to happen next.

'I'm afraid we can't, the money is gone, so for now we'll say that we love it here.'

Not one to like the idea of lying down with the horrors of this new grief, Mary turned her head to public things. She needed to move and do. First she put on her coat and set out to be a volunteer worker in the female refuge, a place for distressed women and children, they told her. It took her some days to know who was there.

'Former prostitutes and unmarried mothers, that's who,' she told Evelyn. She absorbed the truth of it and began to see the world another way. The women here were not bad – unlucky yes, as if God had spilt salt on their lives. She had had some of that herself.

Evelyn settled into her job, being a flume for telegraphs, words travelling by sound on wire, words about all sorts of things: ships arriving, gold being found, children being born, miners revolting. The messages sizzled through, with their Morse overcoats, and she converted them into sentences long enough to be understood. She didn't write home much – she saw little point in exchanging notes about things that could not be known so far away, and less in trying to explain what the task of looking after their mother now included. She tried once to write what Mary had become: the speeches, the letters, the travelling to wild towns, her love of the notion of women with votes. But it looked flat on the page, it couldn't lift into what it was, it couldn't paint the fight. Evelyn was watching a revolt, a fit of fury working itself into reasonable language. It was like nothing she had ever imagined.

Mary joined the women's committee of the Social Purity Society. It fitted well with thoughts she had about making life better for girls, raising the age of consent for one thing. A passer-by, looking at the notice of their meetings, would not have guessed what was being said inside. And when that talk grew into other things, as talk will, looking for the vote seemed not such an outlandish thing – seemed natural really, a small something to upgrade women.

'It's not too much to ask. We had that in the Brehon laws a long time ago,' Mary said.

'What are they?'

'Old Irish. It doesn't matter. Not here anyway.'

They wrote the Women's Suffrage League on a piece of paper and liked the look of it.

'Fair play is a jewel,' she said when she came home.

'Why do you say that?' Evelyn asked, fiddling with her brooch, as she thought about what it might mean.

'I saw famine and what happened. I saw women making their minds up. They sometimes had to decide who would die. If they can do that, they should be able to vote.'

'But some of them don't want the vote,' Evelyn said.

'Ah yes, it has taken centuries to make us the fools we are – it will take time to wade out of our slough.'

Mary still read poetry, when there was time. It gave her the backbone to answer the deluge that sometimes threatened to swamp her after one of her letters. She wrote about a man, one in a righteous rage, who claimed the gospels on his side.

'Will he hold up his hands in holy horror if I tell him that though St Paul's learning is unquestioned, and his inspired doctrine unassailable, his social rules are decidedly behind the age! Who cares whether I had my bonnet on or off while I spoke on Friday? Where was the "shame" if my hair were long or short any more than if it were black or brown or grey?

'Do you think that reply is all right?' Mary asked.

Evelyn wasn't sure, but thought that by now her mother knew what she was doing. Wasn't she already on the road, going to faraway places, getting names written on paper sheets, a petition that would show it wasn't just a few mad women who wanted the vote. She spoke in all sorts of places: Port Augusta, Port Pirie and Quorn.

'That's a funny name, Evelyn, isn't it? Quorn. It's a railway place. There were five hundred at Port Pirie, imagine that.'

Sometimes on her journeys she would see a turn in the road that looked like home, a dead ringer for the road to Ballybay, and she would shake her head and wonder where she was and what she was doing shouting from the back of trailers. It didn't happen often, which was just as well, and coming out of the bend she would see a bleached shade and perhaps an extravagant bird, things that could only be in her new place.

The petition grew in length; the pages began to stack up. Not one signature looked like another. Mary wrote pamphlets as well as letters, which were sent to more and more newspapers, again and again, and to members of parliament and whoever else might do with having their minds changed. She learned the patience for repetition. Unlike others, she could sign her own name publicly, no fears. There had to be some advantages to being a widow, she thought.

'I'll talk to the temperance people too, although I don't trust total abstinence,' she said, getting tired at the idea of it.

The women poured a glass on the night they stuck together the pages of 11,600 penned names, then rolled up the four-hundred-foot-long scroll and tied it with gold ribbon.

Mary dated her letter December 1894 and wrote home that on last Tuesday morning the triumphant cry had gone up from the packed gallery. After years of work, only six in the end, South Australian women had won the right to vote by thirty-one votes to fourteen.

'And it was such a margin too – we're made even more joyous by that,' she said. 'One operator thought to add the right to sit in parliament, thinking that would get the whole shebang scuppered. Oh, how we laughed and cried with joy when it didn't work. Not this time.'

'I wonder what they'll make of that,' Evelyn said, wondering herself what her mother would do now.

One son had no intention of telling anyone what his mother was at; he had always been like that, had let her voice go over his head like a kite disappearing. He looked up a lot. And he'd married a fool of a girl who knew next to nothing. At least not the things Mary knew. The other son was proud enough and knew some people whom he would tell.

'I remember when you were a small boy, you told me your dream one morning but stopped halfway and said, "Oh, no need, you were in it." I had to tell you that your dreams were your own. Only you knew what happened in them. You were happy about that.'

On the morning of the first vote, they turned out in droves, dressed in many colours as well as black. Mary Lee wore her best frock, a crimson shade with familiar ruffles and puffs on the shoulder. Evelyn's dress had a bell-like flow to it. She had bought it thinking that it would suit the new drop-frame bicycle, if she could ever get one. After they'd marked their papers they gathered outside and talked excitedly. Some men snorted as they passed, others pretended not to see them, and yet more doffed their hats and said enthusiastic things like 'Good morning, ladies.'

On their way home Mary said, 'You go ahead,' and Evelyn did, wanting to walk a bit on her own to think about what history is.

Mary Lee found a spot in off the path and lay down under the everlasting sky; no one would find her here. She sighed with gratitude, and thought of all the roads she had taken. The shouting from hall stages might have been easier if she had known that it would indeed succeed. She spoke to her George, as she often did. There was nothing helpless about this, she did it most days. She told him that without his fate she would have been at home, would have had nothing to do with all this, but that she couldn't stay where she had lost him. And that as long as she was here in this bigger place with this bigger thing to do, she could sometimes forget the long missing of him. She told him of what grew on the trees in the backyard – lemons, oranges and the like, not just Armagh apples. She got up and dusted herself off.

And Evelyn was right to wonder what Mary would do next. The fritillaries would have been coming out in her Irish garden on the morning she got ready for Broken Hill. There weren't the same ones here but there was one called snake's head; well, that would make sense, not so much at home of course. Mary had become a campaign sort of soul. At the age of seventy-three she set out, in searing heat, to see what she could do for miners on strike, miners and their families not coated in gold. She would use what she had now learned for another good – there was no reason yet to sleep the day away. The poverty shocked her, there was much to do. She would need to lie down under that sky again, look up into it to shut out the grime.

Evelyn did eventually write the long letter home, when it was necessary to do so. She told them that their mother was buried with Ben, to the left of some lush trees. She would now try to let them know about the last years of her life. She didn't say anything about the lack of money – they would have been surprised by that. She told them about Mary writing in support of children being able to swim naked together. In reply to the outrage, she had written 'I don't believe that Eve ever had petticoats, and if Adam had britches, they left us no pattern – and they were both naked and not ashamed. Does not half the moral dirt of the world spring from dirty suggestion?' Evelyn wondered if her siblings would understand the notion of how heat could cause you to throw your clothes off.

She told them about the unions asking Mary to stand for parliament, an astonishing thing to happen so soon

64

after the vote was achieved. She called her Mary when she wrote these things, not Mother. She explained that Mary declined the request on the grounds that she wanted to work undeterred by allegiance to any party. She explained that when she died people were surprised at her age – they thought her much younger surely. Mary herself hadn't dwelt much on her age but one day she had remarked that she had spent almost the same number of years in Monaghan as here, and neither place knew what she did in the other. Evelyn wrote that she knew then Mary was dying; she had returned to her youth.

'You may find it hard to imagine her, all that dedication, you may not remember any of that from before. Our mother was a great woman, you know.'

Evelyn posted it on her way to work. When the letter dropped into the box, she wondered about writing the last sentence – maybe she should have left it out. It was hard to know what to say really, in the circumstances. And hard to know what road to take herself now. She got back on her new bicycle and pedalled up Wakefield Street, enjoying the breeze that the speed created around her face.

Virgin Birth

The first woman to deliberately become pregnant after the atom bomb was dropped on Hiroshima made love, and was made love to, in a serious fashion. There was little inclination for fripperies. All around them the lily-of-the-valley lanterns were gone; they were in the past, like all the houses and the street pavements and the offices and the schools, although already some teachers, who were left, were taking the children, who were left, for classes under the trees that were not left, because teachers are like that. The war was over too, but only just, and that was not a thing to be believed readily. This woman's greatest joy was that she had the nerve to do this, kick into making love, and her greatest hope was that once she had taken this leap the word would spread. The man was shocked to discover that his fear and his sadness and the empty hole where he had thought he had a heart all came together to strengthen his body quite deliberately. He was, too, shocked and pleased almost to the point of tears, when the woman appeared to fill up with startled joy. She felt herself become pregnant, knew that the egg had split – it sent a quiver to her ribcage and she screamed with delicious fright. The man may have felt it also – he certainly felt her strive to take every ounce of the soul and body of him into her.

I was on my way to see her, to see if all this was true, and to find out if she would tell me. Sixty years later and from an island on the same latitude west, or as same as makes no difference. There would be little amusement about this journey. I was being sent by my university, or so I said. In truth I had chosen to do this, the same way as I had chosen to go to Oradour-sur-Glane – I had given up telling my friends about the memorials that I had voluntarily visited, and given up telling them that you do not stop children making noise or doing hopscotch on the most intricate light work that took years to design. Watching them not know things can console greatly.

On the night before I left, they and I went drinking, although this was not what I wanted to do. The air was gay, all the people were shouting happy, it was only me, distracted by my task in hand, who felt the paper-thinness of the evening. And I was afraid that I would not be able to come back to this light-heartedness. But I should have known not to have such a worry. Hadn't I come back from Oradour and after a week or so, or a month or two maybe, hadn't I almost forgotten the feel of that July morning? Hadn't I stopped seeing the men making hay, the pitchforks catching occasional glints of sun, stopped smelling the bread that some women were making? After some time I could hear no sounds of children cracking in the air. I had stopped wondering what the animals did when they heard so many thundering bangs, and smelt the smoke of the church with the women and the children in it, and heard the screams, because there must have been screams. I had stopped wondering too if the women, before the church was set on fire, knew that the men were dead. Had they felt it their bones? Had they lied, as women will to children, and told them that everything would be all right?

I went home early, to pack I said, but I already had everything in the suitcase and all my documents in a light bag, including my Japan Rail Pass with the big wave on it, my language book, which was there merely as a token of glancing effort, my yen safely tucked in my wallet and my passport checked too often, as if the expiry date might have changed in the middle of the night. I went to bed and slept. I had a long-necked dream and was glad to waken out of it. I got the blue bus out through the wakening city and went through security at the airport. If anyone had noticed me, they could have thought I was going on an ordinary holiday.

I accomplished the flight in the way that I presume is normal, with moments of sheer bafflement, followed by hours of understandable boredom. At heart I feel that one should be conscious of enormity at all times on an aeroplane journey. I tried to surreptitiously examine the staff, the look and gestures of them, the gracious bowing. Could one get angry while still bowing? By the time we touched down in Tokyo I was almost used to the ideas in my head.

I stayed overnight in a hotel that I had booked. I had not been prepared for the confusion of sights and sounds. It felt like an enormous accomplishment to get inside the door. The effort of checking in had exhausted me so much that I fell into a deep sleep when I lay down on the bed, only vaguely aware of the sound of piped music as it heralded the train into the nearby station. I had been told that I could recognise the stations by the music played – I wasn't sure that I would trust that piece of information.

In the morning I looked out the window to watch the shapes of walking people, the way they did not bump into each other although they did not seem to look at those around them. I made my way downstairs, had breakfast in a sedate, leisurely manner and found my way to the station and the correct platform. I was ready to board a train for Hiroshima. I continually glanced at the noticeboard to make sure that this was real, that I could be going to this place. I boarded as one would any other train, wondering if I looked like a person going to Hiroshima. We pulled out of the station slowly, the train gradually picking up speed, racing past ugly snakes of buildings, the eye relieved only occasionally by the tantalising glimpse of a temple, an old-fashioned house or a field. It drew into Hiroshima station on time.

After alighting, I stood on the platform for some time, checking my senses, because there are places that are hard to believe and they need to be looked at with care. Again, I was going to a hotel. I had the name well rehearsed but it didn't work. The taxi driver patiently tried this and that and then clapped his hands, he had it. He looked to be over seventy so would have been born then. As he drove down the road, I looked at the trees. Were they new? Of course they were new. Everything was new, under sixty, every single thing, except for this driver. When he pulled up outside the hotel, I momentarily became panicked about the protocol of tipping. It would be terrible to do the wrong thing to this man.

At the desk I foresaw drama of some sort, but my check-in was accomplished with flurries of good humour that I had not expected. I would have to loosen my clothes and bones. These people knew something that I didn't, how to reinhabit ruins, this is maybe why they laughed. A sports team of young men lined up at the door. Their shiny T-shirts were emblazoned with carp and the receptionist pointed excitedly at them and told me something.

The room was small, the bath was for sitting in with knees up, there was an ashtray and a notice asking me not to smoke in bed. Everything was clean. I slept off some residual jet lag as the sun began to go down and woke suddenly an hour later into a striped darkness in the room. I hurried out to the street and ventured to eat by pointing at pictures on a menu in the window.

The next morning, brighter and slept, I walked to the Peace Memorial Park. There was nothing normal about the walk. I noticed every tree, heard every bird, as if I were frozen in another minute decades ago. When they planted the first tree, afterwards, did a bird fly in to sit on it, to signal to them that they were right? And how far had the bird come? Around me people drove cars and walked about, bought and sold items in shops. If you had a tree or a baby here you would boast about it.

I have always closed my eyes after a day in a new place to check if it was as I imagined it would be, but as soon as I stepped through the door of the Peace Memorial Museum, I lost any previous picture. I have tried often since then but nothing comes. Instead, I am left with what I actually saw. Or fragments of it, because the mind generally has a safety shutdown valve. Different images come at different times so I am not overwhelmed. I do remember the photograph at the entrance. It is of a blue blue sky, one bird seemingly gliding through it as if it owned it, which indeed it did. It is comforting to think of that and to know that it would have treated the sunny day with gratitude; it would not have seen the perfect light as a reason to choose this spot to become notorious.

There had been a list of possible targets but the cloudless morning sealed Hiroshima's fate. The minutes of the meeting are concise. An atomic bomb should be used 'on a war plant surrounded by workers' houses, and that it would be used without prior warning'. You cannot have post prior warning. But the commas were in their correct place. An earlier ordinary bomb warning was cleared and so the maximum number of people were hurrying to work and school, going on with life as we do, even during war, either because we do not have the sense to fall to our knees and wail at the sky or because we have done that and found it to be useless.

The plane came over at 8.15 a.m. The pilot is reported to have said that if Dante had been with them, he would have been terrified. Is this true? Did a pilot who knew Dante do this? There is an aerial photograph showing a smudge on a river that was a city, a two kilometre radius of melted wasteland where minutes ago there had been a city of people. I closed my eyes and measured a two kilometre radius in my head, from Duffy's to McCabe's to Kavanagh's and back. A few walls stand laughingly erect in the picture. Below them people have jumped into the river which is, too, on fire. We cannot see them. I caught up with a school tour and rowed behind them safely until I got to the exit. The teenagers were quiet and I wondered what they would take away with them to their village in the mountains. Would they be able to shut out the pictures of dripping skin, would they remember the words A-bomb microcephaly, or would they instead see the toys that had been saved in the outer suburbs? Would the act of making them see all this help towards the midwifery of sanity? Outside I lit a cigarette and listened to ordinary noises. It was a while before I could hear conversation. A woman asked her husband if that had been Italy on the map, no no, the Philippines, he whispered, looking around with a shamed face, and although I was horrified, I also thought, at least she came. I was relieved that the children could not understand this geography lesson. The woman tossed her head and said 'that was a good picture of Truman'.

I trailed myself to the Children's Monument where other school tours waited their turn, bowed to their teachers and sang songs. I turned away. I stopped at the Hair Monument, where a brief poem declared, 'We enshrine here hair,/ Cut and gathered in the morn of life.' If the school tours stopped here would the boys and girls touch their black, polished heads? I walked on towards the hotel, looking back once to the bridge.

There are two ground zeros in the world, here and Nagasaki. Poor Nagasaki; had they heard the news and were they afraid?

I went to my room and slept.

In the morning I reluctantly had miso and sushi for breakfast as I waited for my arranged guide to pick me up. I wondered what this building had been, before, and if it had been a hotel was this the lobby and what paintings had hung here? Flowering plum blooms, rose mallows fashioned from gold leaf, mournful autumn gingko leaves? Or if there had been a black and gold lacquerware box sitting in the window, which of the hundred layers of lacquer melted first? Ken'ichi Iwata came quickly to the door to collect me. I bowed in all the correct places having learned now how to do it, or so I hoped. He was cheerful and I understood his perfect English, 'Now we will go to see the people you wish to interview.'

The woman, who was perhaps eighty years old – that would be just about right – smiled at me a lot. Here was the woman who had shown the most hope imaginable in the world. There was a man with her, probably also eighty. I wanted to ask if this was the man but I couldn't. There was much ceremony about making the tea. I would have liked to help, but when I tried to raise myself from the chair shouts and little screams made me sit again. The translator and my hosts talked a lot, he occasionally bursting into English to let me know what was going on. That weather forecaster was no good – last spring he had not predicted the day of the blossoming of the cherry trees correctly, they had missed the best bit. Well, they did see some of them but the best bit is the first day. How was my journey? Was I tired? The translator said that he was born in the year of the dog and so he liked to do his rounds every morning, was it possible to still do that in Dublin? It had been, when he was there learning English. We waited to get to the subject of my visit, but the longer we waited and the more conversation we threaded through the translator and the more smiling we did, the less it seemed appropriate. So, I talked of our spring and of what winter is like, and when we have snow. I told them about our few meagre cherry blossoms, and what our weather forecasters talk about and soon it was time to go. I bowed and bowed and bowed my way out to the translator's car. The woman and the man both stood at the door waving to me. The translator and I did not refer to our conversation. On the journey back I noticed that my fingernails had grown.

Two things happened the day I left Japan. Paul Tibbets died, the man with the ordinary name, the man who knew who Dante was. He had three sons, a number of grandchildren, one a B-2 bomber, and great-grandchildren. They are all well as far as we know. He had named the plane for his mother and the bomb he called Little Boy. He had finished his days running an air taxi service after he had retired from the air force. The *Japan Times* was happy to report that, although they did not know what it meant. It also reported that an opera diva had spoken out about the bamboo ceiling that prevented Asian singers getting roles. Villagers beside Mount Kelud in Indonesia, which was rumbling ferociously, had decided to stay put and follow the local myth of not lighting lights and not speaking in loud voices, as a way of helping the mountain not to erupt. The last thing that happened before I boarded the plane, to take the Siberian route home, was that the Waterford Glass Cup was presented at the Tokyo races.

The following Friday evening I met my friends again. Presumably I looked the same as I had the last time, which just goes to show how little one can trust looks. We settled into the night.

'Not appropriate! You what? You went all the way to Japan and didn't talk about it.'

'No. It didn't seem right.'

My friends in the bar looked at me for a moment, wondering what they could speak about next. They made an effort not to look at each other, in case I saw them thinking something about me.

Disturbing Words

I know you're wondering what I'm doing up here, not just up here, but here at all, the last you'd heard I was away out foreign someplace. So foreign that you don't even know the name of it, and that's a hard enough thing to achieve these days, when there is always some lurker beside you with infinite information on his telephone, as well as his entire life. Infinite does mean that there's no end to it, which is never a good thing. You mention a place, the strangeness of it lovingly on your tongue, its faraway mysteries tucked into the silence that you're trying to leave around it, and your man has whipped out his gadget. 'How do you spell that?' he bellows. Perhaps not bellows, but it feels like it, the roaring cult of the amateur know-all. Your youth was gloriously lived with the photographs kept in an album and only taken out if there was a reason to do so, something to check or an emigrant visiting, something to do with them when the talk of their grown children and their new fridge had run out of steam.

Actually, in all honesty, it's so long since you heard

the last of me I could have been dead. And you're right, I have been away in a peculiar place, almost desert really, a place with red earth, spindly bits of mangy grass and heat that is laughable. And a neighbour whose job is building underground car parks in mosques.

But I had come home for my parents' funeral, naturally. And I say home when I'm here because it's easier. Demanding that anyone call my air-conditioned desert pad home would be a bit much. My parents had died within a day of each other and, luckily enough, the first funeral hadn't taken place so the two wakes were held together. In the passing around of the word it got mixed up which of them had gone first but it didn't really matter. Not to outsiders anyway. It did to me. But over the few days, the more I accepted condolences, even I got confused as to which of them had died of the broken heart. But I could have worked it out by trying to remember who was named when my phone went in Abu Dhabi. Because I was on my way home, after hearing about the first, when they rang to tell me about the second. I had thought that they were just checking to see how my flights were going so far, no delays, that sort of thing.

On the first evening after the coffins were got and all the other essentials seen to, the neighbours came in with their manners and their good thoughts, and after some sadness they proceeded to garden the memories so that there could be a shape put on the next few days. And a discreet map made for themselves, one to move on with next week. Before the day was up, between us we'd have looked at a lot of things about the lives of my parents, how they had met, and although we wouldn't say it, how love had changed them.

'They're pulling from our pen now,' my father's oldest friend, John Moloney, said.

He had meant it to be heard only over in the corner where the slagging men had gathered. But there had been a bit of quiet and it travelled further into the room. Brian Gallagher bristled. He wasn't too well himself at the minute. Mrs Clancy jumped in with sandwiches and the talk took up again.

For as long as they could remember, my father was a pernickety sort of man, particularly around language, and my mother seemed to follow suit. Although some of the women weren't sure if the following suit was a sleight of hand, they thought that it might have been her who started it. She was known as a reader. Serious reading hid in her very nerves. She got terribly annoyed about the man who had come walking here when he was writing a book. He had lied about things she had told him. When she brought it up with the women, they could see that it mattered more to her than it did to them.

'Imagine pretending when there was no need to,' she said indignantly. 'As if we wouldn't find out, as if we didn't read on the border.' They nodded their heads towards her. She spoke the truth.

And now they were gathered, talking their ways through the shock of them both gone.

'Remember the time he dressed you down for saying UK?' someone called to Gerry Moore. And Gerry, who was a perfect mimic, brought my father's voice straight into the room.

'Let's not get lazy, it's England, or Britain if you want. United Kingdom of Great Britain and Northern Ireland? Not around here. And as for an Ulster Scot, that's a Monaghan woman in Edinburgh. Scotch Irish, that's how it goes. If we mind our language the rest will follow.'

And we all stayed quiet in honour of the man who had

thought that language mattered and the woman who liked the sound of the truth.

My father had been hurt young by the border; the line ran on the top of their ditch. His mother had mourned the loss of her friends, from both sides of the house.

'That's making them from a different country. How could that be?' She stopped to think about it some more. 'So, if you were born in the six counties before now where will they say you are from? You can't have been from somewhere that never was.'

She looked out some more over the imaginary divide, as people have always done, that is people who have lived on borders, who have heard the river running from one place to the other, not hesitating as it crosses the line.

'But you haven't lost them,' my grandfather said. 'You'll just have to go through a checkpoint to see them.'

'You'd soon get tired of that,' she said, looking over to the field, third from the window, that would now be in a different country.

Now that it had been mentioned, I remembered the day that Gerry had got dressed down. They were moving cattle from the field that had all the grass eaten. This always caused a problem because they had to manoeuvre the cows over territory that had been disputed. In other places, moving cattle caused problems because of cars coming around a bend too fast and landing on top of you, or a cow throwing back her head with the freedom of the road and making a run for it. They had all had a great time over at the Forkhill Singers' weekend. The pub had been lit up with sound. Singers had come from all over the country as well as England, Scotland, Wales, the Isle of Man. The songs had happened, tied in with each other, ebbing and flowing all night. It could have been thought to be a funny thing, grown men and women hanging on to the words of songs. But if you were there you could see the sense of it. It would appear that at some stage Gerry had gone outside and found a soldier with his ear up to a secluded back window, lost in an air from his own place. Those of us who know that can never forget it.

After the cattle had been successfully got into the new field, and had disappeared in a cloud of joy to its far corners of shining abundant grass, the conversation slid into border things. It must have been the songs that did it, or Gerry seeing the soldier and feeling sad for him, because they were usually careful to leave that sort of talk for behind their own closed doors. And somehow or another things got out of hand and descended into a shouting match and the evening became known as that time of the big row, a singular description, out on its own, the big row. Some of it carried across the fields, so we know about bits of it, but other things were said that passers-by couldn't hear. My father came home quiet.

That shouting had been the end of something or the beginning of something else. My father left the modern world, stopped listening to the news. Funny enough, my mother didn't, but then women can be like that, just in case there's the equivalent of a washing machine being developed, and they'd need to know. And in her case, something being written that might make sense of things. In time though, she too said that there wasn't much of use going on and she retreated from the radio, back to her books. She did get a mobile phone but she didn't charge it up that often. They ate their dinner quietly, making happy little remarks about the taste of things.

And I began to know that I would go away.

Around here they were all good at going away. The town

down the road was so dead it didn't even know it. Gerry said that even country and western singers wouldn't darken the door of what passed for the pub, although, mind you, things were cheerful enough in the one on the actual border, the one where the real singing had been. They had lots to laugh at there – the Traynor boys being caught smuggling a load of drink in an ambulance that they'd bought and converted, the Murtagh boys having their load taken off them by customs men who turned out not to be customs men at all, but maybe the Traynor boys dressed up. They concentrated on those bits, not serious things, only matters of money.

Yes, I had gone away. First to Dublin, where they couldn't stop hearing the headlines in my accent, and then to further away where it didn't matter. And as soon as the next plate of sandwiches was handed around maybe I'd go away again, slip out the door and up the lane. Or at least start packing my bag to the murmur of them in the kitchen.

Before I left for the faraway place my mother had said, always live away from the border.

On the second morning of the wakes, I took a breath and opened the desk in the back bedroom; I would take a very quick look. I had no notion of going through things, all that could wait. But the tidy bundle, strung together with a loose hessian bow, on the very top of all else, was clearly meant to be looked at. I was so glad that my brother hadn't come yet, not until this afternoon. My mother would have hated his suburban wife going through her things, not understanding what they meant, trying to put a value on them.

I undid the twine and spread out the papers. There were pages and pages of meticulous notes on all things border.

All things to do with the partition of Ireland. Who had mentioned it first. How it had come about that it was six counties and not four. And which six. There were notes on the Border Commission and chapters of books photocopied. There was a fortnight's reading in it, even for the first skim. One page had a large printing of the word *gerrymander*. It was my mother's handwriting below it. It stated that gerrymander was first used in the nineteenth century in the *Boston Weekly Messenger*, referring to the new voting district that Governor Elbridge Gerry had carved out to favour his own party, the map of which resembled a salamander. Behind that was a picture of my parents at the filling in of the cratered roads, those blown up by the British army. You could see them happening in the look they were giving each other. A split second of light between the trees, their futures hovering together. This was now where they wanted to be. They'd met, apparently, on the third day of the filling in. My grandmother must have loved that. At least something good would come out of it. As they worked, some of the photographers caught shadows of soldiers passing along the hedges. The people didn't hate soldiers yet but they would if needs be. And in time they learned how to look out the car window, straight ahead, silent, as the camouflaged men with blackened faces examined their driving licences.

And there was my first letter to them from the desert. On the back of the envelope was a tiny map that I couldn't make out, the writing was so small, but there was our barn door, and all sorts of lines drawn down from it. It took me some time to find the larger version, which turned out to be a perfectly precise architectural flourish. My father and mother had drawn a plan to build a basement that would cross the border and thus they would live in two places. I wanted to believe that telling them about the underground car park in the mosque had helped. I really wanted to believe it. But in the meantime, there was the tree. There was a picture of it, pinned to pages and more pages of horticultural notes. Clearly, they had cultivated the tree to make sure that its roots, and now its branches, would spread across the line. I was struck still by the amusement of it all. Who would ever have thought of it?

I heard movements begin as the morning started and I was needed downstairs but first I had to check the barn. I would slip out before the serious day began. I pushed open the door, multicoloured in layers of new paints gone old. I fumbled my way to the far corner and there it was, a velvet curtain hanging as if in front of a stage, covering a large opening. Just for a few seconds I heard a ghost tapping sound, a small noise as the job was begun, and then a bigger one as the larger pick was used. I stared down into the darkness and wanted to see how far they'd got but heard my name being called, again. Later would do.

During the actual funeral, the parts that are said to remind us of the end, I thought of their beginning together and could dimly hear their laughs in chorus, as they drew to their hearts' content. So that's what they'd done when they left the news behind.

We were saying goodbye to some of the mourners when we saw the big yellow machine negotiate its way through the gap of the field on the other side, over the bog, up the hill. We watched as it stationed itself, belching out bad fumes. A cutting device unfolded and edged towards the tree. I don't quite know what got into me but I ran for it and made up through the branches as if I did this sort of thing every day. There was no thinking about how to get up a tree, no thinking about why, and what after. I had never known that I had such speed, nor that I could climb so high. The men roared at the machine and soon the driver saw me, perched up on the top, and he withdrew the blades. So here I am. With no plan.

I have plenty of time to think, although you'd be surprised how much there is to do. I have to organise the food, and other things, that they send up to me on a pulley that Gerry made in jig time. Eating takes a bit of work; it's not like I'm sitting in a kitchen. It's amazing what you can see from up here, how the people organise their days, how they move about, where they hide their scrap, how people sometimes break into dance in their kitchens. Although in the first few days it would be hard to know if perhaps they didn't change their routine, open their curtains earlier than normal. But that could have been to look at me. I'm also sure that George Wiggins never put out a flag every day before this.

Between myself and the people below we've decided that if I can manage to stay long enough the point will be made and they'll leave the tree alone. That's the general idea.

The big question now is, what is long enough, when do I come down? I do have a life waiting for me, with friends in it, and I will eventually need to be in a place where I am not known as the person who went up the tree that went over the border.

I did come down. And went back to the desert where we had a party and discussed borders we had crossed. And Famagusta, the sound of the name and the ghosts whistling through the deserted city. Cancer, the equator, Capricorn. One of us had stood with women shouting to their relatives across to Jordan. The remark was made that the proximity of the border had had a serious effect on Anselm Kiefer. What about Alsace-Lorraine? Back and forth, back and forth. Korea, we said. Another of us, a tent maker, had had more truck than most with borders. He had seen a lot of people looking over lines. He told us that while the rest of us forget, get distracted by newer tragedies, the people forced to move often take excursions to look back.

When the sun dropped down and the barbecue was over no one could remember how the conversation had got started. I get occasional cards from home and apparently the tree has not been touched, and Gerry spends a lot of time in our barn.

Reasons I Know of That We Are Not Allowed to Speak to Our Grandmother

It began with me having to do an essay for school about my grandmother. Only some of us were asked to do it. It was for a competition for a visiting writer who was coming to our class the following month.

'Is that all he does, sir, write?' a boy asked.

'Yes, that's what he is, a writer, just like your father is an actuary, I believe.'

That may have been the first time the boy had a name for what his father was.

Those of us who were chosen made a show of huffing and puffing and told the others that they were lucky, but secretly I was pleased. The essay was to be about how the old spent their Saturday nights. Mr McGrane was particularly interested in how those who lived alone fared on such a busy evening. He must have chosen those of us who had grannies on their own, maybe it was not because we were good at essays. We could concentrate on aspects of loneliness. Were they more poignant in contrast to the fullness of the clamour and clatter of a Saturday night? P O I G N A N T. We could look it up in the dictionary. And while we were at it, we could find out the difference between 'bathos' and 'pathos'. The ones who weren't chosen laughed at that and some of them pointed their fingers at us. Mr McGrane saw that, and said everyone had to look up the words.

'And I would like you to stick as near to the truth as possible,' he said.

It was this commandment that made me niggle my father over and over again that evening and the next day to bring me to our grandmother's at nine o'clock on Saturday night. This was not a time that we would normally visit her. I had decided on nine o'clock because I thought that the loneliness mentioned by Mr McGrane would have set in by then, and I'd be able to see it for myself, without my grandmother or my father knowing what I was up to.

When we arrived at the door she wasn't in and my father seemed annoyed by this. We puttered about for a while but she didn't come back.

'Are you sure Mr McGrane meant you to be so precise? Seems more like a report to me than an essay. Surely an essay should be more imaginative.'

I hated it when my father got all know-all like that. As if he knew better than my teacher. I said, bolstered by the order to accuracy, 'Yes.'

'Oh well then, we'd better look for her, I suppose,' my father said.

We went next door to my grandmother's neighbour, an old woman who scared me the way that I think grandmothers are maybe meant to, but which mine didn't. My father asked her if she might know where my grandmother was.

'What time is it? That blooming clock is never right.'

This struck me as odd; surely there would be more than one clock in the house. Ours had at least four that I could think of at this minute. Maybe I would put in the essay that my grandmother's neighbour had only one clock and it was always wrong.

'It's eh … let me see …' and my father pulled back the sleeve of his jacket to look at his watch, which had a purple face. I could hear a baby crying in the house on the other side. 'Half past nine now,' he said.

'Half past nine on a Saturday night. Well, she'll have her feet well up back in Slatterys by now. Slatterys, you know, the pub.'

My father closed his face. You have to know him well to see him doing that. I know him well, or at least the bits of him that I notice.

'Slatterys, the pub,' she said again, putting the emphasis on the last word.

'Yes. Yes,' my father said, tetchily, and my grandmother's neighbour chuckled.

'What did she mean, *back* in Slatterys?' I asked when we were in the car.

'Oh, she's from the west, they say back with everything.'

My father sounded cross. I was only trying to get him to open his face again.

Maybe if we hadn't gone to the pub it would have been all right. He parked the car in a sullen manner. I would need to look that up too with the bathos word. I hear words and like them but sometimes use them in the wrong place. He said 'stay there' unnecessarily. Even I knew that children were not allowed in pubs after nine o'clock at night. There had been an uproar about it which I couldn't understand.

What could happen that you would have to have a child in a pub after nine o'clock at night? And what was the difference between a pub and a bar? I hadn't brought my book with me; we had, after all, only been going to visit our grandmother. There was nothing to read in the car except some scraps, but they did all right.

My father came out from the pub a few minutes later – I'm not sure exactly how long he was in there but I hadn't got bored. He was fuming. That word is definitely correct. I thought it best not to talk on the way home.

I was sent to bed the minute we got in, unreasonably early, I thought. Later, as the noise from the kitchen got louder, I left my room and sat on the top of the stairs. There is always a child on the stairs, otherwise how would we learn.

'You want to see the crowd she was with.'

'Did you know any of them?'

'Not one. And the way she– '

'Tell me again what she said,' my mother interrupted, sounding as if she wanted to put the answer out flat on the table and examine it the way she did before she sewed something.

'She said that I should be grateful she had a life and wasn't sitting at home alone moping about. She said that I had no business checking up on her, that she'd had enough constriction when she was rearing me.'

'Are you sure it was *constriction* she said?'

'Yes I'm sure,' my father ground out. 'I would hardly make it up.'

'And did she really ask you to leave?' my mother asked in her kind voice.

'Well as good as.'

The conversation went on like this for a long time, sounding liked turned-down music or distant wind, but I couldn't follow it really and also, I did get bored because I couldn't understand what they were getting so exercised about. You can use that word as a description. It does not mean that they have been running or swimming all night.

On Monday when Mr McGrane asked me how the essay was going, I said 'fine'.

It was very soon after that our grandmother arrived at our house full of high dudgeon – I love when I can think that's what people are in. I'm almost certain if the pub episode had not happened, we would not have got that visit. This time I was out in the garden, and although my father closed the door – now that I think of it, already not prepared to let things return to normal – I moved up to the back wall and sat down under the open window. My older sister was getting married, next year I think. There was a lot of fuss, even already, I'd heard my mother saying. Sometimes it would last for an entire hour but then it would die down for days. Sometimes there would be the word wedding, wedding, wedding blowing up all over the place. And then there would be weeks when no one at all mentioned the circus, as my mother called it. I didn't care about the ins and outs of it, but I presumed it would be interesting to be a part of it on the actual day. It was also a very long way away so I could see no reason to think about it yet. So, it surprised me that our grandmother arrived so early to discuss it. Although I'm sure this could not really be called a discussion.

'As you are well aware, I have no interest in ribbons, so clearly I'll be having some trouble with this,' our grandmother said. She must then have thrown something on the table, a letter or a card. I don't know if she gave my parents time to finish reading it – there was quiet for a very short time.

'Now, I know that there are sewers in the world, people who sew' – even I knew that this was a dig at my mother – 'but they don't have to stick needles into everything.'

'Just a minute,' my father said.

'Yes,' our grandmother said, letting the word turn up at the end, as if it was a question or being said by an Australian.

'Just a minute,' my father repeated, 'this is no way to talk to my wife.'

'Oh for heaven's sake, Liam, your *what*? She has a name, and actually I'm not just talking to Gertrude, I'm talking to you too. You may not be allowed to say that your daughter has lost the complete run of herself but I can. I will not, I repeat, will not, be told by anyone what to wear, and no one will ask me to put a ribbon on a hat. Who said I was going to wear a hat anyway?'

'I don't think she meant it like that,' my mother said.

'And may I ask what way you think she meant it? This is quite clear. An order to wear a specific colour so that I can fit into some ludicrous pattern that this young one has in mind.'

'But is there anything wrong with the colours matching on the day?' my mother asked.

My father had gone quiet.

'No, indeed there's not, if it so happens that they do. But that's the point, if it so happens.' Clearly our grandmother was trying to show some interest but I could tell that she didn't care about colours at all.

And just then my father piped up, 'This isn't about colours at all, is it Mother? This is about your attitude to marriage.'

Whoa, that was some leap.

I could feel the silence, even outside, and the leg that was under my other one went funny.

'Maybe you're right,' our grandmother finally said. 'If you must know, and I think you're old enough now to be able to bear it, I do have serious difficulties with marriage. I think it's something that should be done privately and not particularly referred to again unless legally necessary.'

She sounded as if she was on a home run.

'If you remember, I never referred to your father as my husband until he died, and if you'll care to remember, this had no bearing on what I felt about or for him.'

'Your trouble is that you have no respect for tradition,' my father said.

'Tradition my arse.'

'Look, there's no need to be so rude.'

'Oh grow up, that's not being rude.'

It was funny hearing someone tell my father to grow up. I had to scratch myself so that I wouldn't be found under the window.

There was a moment's silence, as if our grandmother realised the futility of it all. I had looked up 'futility' the night before. It sounded too as if they were all waiting to see who would go next.

My mother then said, 'Could you not just–' but our grandmother interrupted in a soft voice, 'No, I could not just anything. This is what principle means. Someone has to stand up to this …' She didn't finish the sentence, as if even she knew the next word out of her mouth could be too dangerous.

'And as for tradition, these days anything can be made up into it. It could be something started five years ago. Any old gobshite in a bar could tell them it was always done and they'd believe him.'

'You'd know all about that.'

I didn't know if it was fair of my father to say that. Our

91

grandmother then changed her voice into the sort of one that my mother sometimes uses on us, only us. It comes from outside the sound of normal conversation.

'In this tradition of yours,' our grandmother said, 'I see that maternal respect has got the push.'

It sounded as if she was just at the beginning of her sentence but my father interrupted in the voice that he uses on the telephone if someone rings from work – everyone was changing voices now – 'I'm sorry you feel like that. Do you want a lift anywhere?'

I could hear him coming towards the window so I had to creep my way across to the hedge and slip behind the coal shed away out of sight. It's not used as a coal shed any more since we got the natural gas. Everything is thrown into it. I didn't hear the car leaving.

At teatime the faces were all closed.

And that night when I went out on the stairs, I could hear a real ding-dust of a shouting match. When their voices get that way, they wouldn't notice me even if they tripped over me. The shoutings all ran into each other and it was hard to make out where one began and the other ended, but I did hear plainly my mother saying, 'Your mother was always the same. Happy away up there on her high horse. I'm not surprised she has ended up ...' I couldn't hear the next bit. 'And as for these views of hers. Always superior in her mind to everyone else. Could never have the same look on things as everyone else. Oh no, Miss Precious.' She was talking about our grandmother!

'There was no call for that, no call at all,' my father shouted.

I had to agree with him. I heard a door slamming, saw a slice of light land on the banisters and knew that someone was going to make towards the hall, and in truth too I had decided that it was best for me to hear no more anyway. I slid my bottom across the linoleum into my bedroom. My mother had changed all the upstairs carpet for linoleum – I liked the colour of that word – she said it was healthier. You could never tell the connections that some people make, they must think a lot to come up with them.

The following weekend I was taken away by my parents to the west and we all had a very smooth time, people holding hands and all that.

On Monday Mr McGrane asked me how the essay was going and I said 'fine sir'. He also said that, in the opinion of some, 'Wittgenstein tried to destroy philosophy because he could not understand it. There is no point in destroying something if you don't know what it is. Then again, for many, that's why they destroy things, precisely because they do not know their worth. I hope you got that. Some of you may need to know it. And he destroyed Mr Russell too.' Whoever he was.

I am already a perhaps sort of person. Perhaps everything would have gone completely back to normal if my essay had not won the competition. And been printed in the local paper. Oh shite. I can say that out loud because my parents seem to have too much else on their minds to notice and to reprimand me. I got a postcard from my grandmother congratulating me and that seems to have let all hell loose altogether. But my father did say yesterday, 'See, I told you an imaginative approach is always best.' The fact that he referred to it at all makes me think that his face might open again, and that I'll be able to speak to my grandmother some day soon.

The Reading of It

The air outside had the tease of spring, faint, ever so faint, like the faraway goat's bell in a Swiss mountain story. If you put your nose up you could get a whiff of the jasmine planted by our neighbour, him hoping to be just that little bit above the rest of us. He had more of those thoughts up his sleeve and could be seen tossing them around in that pointy head of his. Anyone could get the smell of jasmine, but you could miss daffodils if you didn't come from country stock, because it takes a lot of them, an entire congregation you might say, to give off any kind of smell. There's a girl in a Jamaica Kincaid story, a Caribbean islander. She was au pair for a couple in New York, so white they could almost be seen through. The woman of the house thought she was being kind, and kept telling her of the great surprise she had in store for her, next week, tomorrow, today. Yes, it's today. She took her to the park, made her close her eyes at the gates, led her in and then whispered, 'Open. Now. Look, oh look, the daffodils, aren't they just so beautiful.'

'I hate daffodils,' the girl said, and she did, because, back home in school, they had been made to learn too many daffodil poems, even though they'd never seen the flower. Their old coloniser had thought it a good plan. After independence, the new rulers hadn't got around to changing the curriculum – these things can't be done overnight. No daffodils grew on her island. 'I hate daffodils,' she said again, but then looked closer, with interest, because she'd never thought they'd look like that. A lot of fuss over a very small flower.

I was thinking about these things, and probably changing them a bit, because I'd been cajoled by another neighbour, three doors up from the man with the jasmine, into her writing class. I live in what you might call a mixed enough area, moved to it when I became a widower, in the hope perhaps of assuaging some pain. The young woman had started giving writing classes in the library and she wanted to get the numbers up, is what she told me. But because of the way I can see people tossing things about in their heads, I knew she was looking for someone different from the run-of-the-mill student, not someone who wanted to be a writer – the time for that clearly having passed. Someone older, in other words; someone who had experiences that the others would be hard put to dream up. Calm, wise experiences, not too modern. Because she often got bits and pieces for me in the local shop if I wasn't feeling well, and because she's a good girl, I said I'd go. I was working my way through her suggested reading list, hence the Jamaica Kincaid.

On the first evening I took the shortcut to the library, through the recycling yard. I met old man Dinkin, although I had no right to think of him thus, the adjective applying just as much to me as to him. We talked a bit about this and that, the local court case that had just finished. We didn't go into the details of it, because it was of a private nature, and we didn't like to talk of such things, but we discussed the characters of the men involved, or at least the characters that the newspapers had given us. He delayed me with some other stories of little consequence, I was only half listening. I had wanted to cut him short but would have felt odd telling him I was going to a class. I knew there were lonely parts to his life, not helped by the fact that his son had married a blatherskite, thereby making it difficult for them to see much of each other.

Eventually I hustled myself away, speeded up a little, but not so much as would make me pant. There's nothing worse than arriving into a classroom out of breath. I was only a few minutes late. The teacher looked up when I sidled in and I felt young again. When I saw her up there she was only a slip of a thing really, and yet she had a stature that surprised me.

She stood, pushed her glasses up her nose and looked at us in a vague sort of way, as if she had more important things than us to think about. In this room she really was not my neighbour. She joined her hands together and made a cone of them. You'd never see her doing that on the street. She welcomed us all, told us we'd get to know each other better as the weeks went on, but it was a good time, before that happened, to really get down to it. And the first thing she asked us to write was a day of our lives, but as a different self, she said. As if I'd dream of doing it any other way. I'd thought about this before, when I read in the newspaper about the Iranian poet, Fatemeh Ekhtesari, who had got eleven-and-a-half years jail and ninety-nine lashes for writing something and meaning something else. I had wondered then how anyone could tell what her original intention had been, how that could be gauged. I have an interest in legal intent because of part of my past life. Well past now, so well past I don't mention it because people can look at an old person and wonder are they making it all up. They see the tattered cloak upon a stick and none of the colour.

Because of the nature of my job, I had met people from all over the world, most of them with their own peculiar expressions, the sound of which made them feel at home. Once, when I was away with work, I met a man who thought like me. It's not every day that happens, so I was glad when we occasionally overlapped again. His sister wrote to me, some months after the last time we'd seen each other, to tell me that he had gone out to the bush to die. I thought about the decision in that, the need to be alone with nature which forgives nothing, but with the joy of watching how birds live. They never look depressed; that should help with dying. I tried to remember how this man had described things. There are different ways of saying you're mad busy. You can say flat out like a lizard drinking; as busy as a one-armed paper-hanger with piles; or fucked to a feather like Mooney's linnet, if you really want to unsettle the listeners.

The variety of people I had met gave me an open view of the world – how could it be otherwise – and I took that feeling with me when I retired to my present street, although I didn't advertise it. But that's why I don't fly off into conniptions when someone, usually a young man, does something out of place. There's a voice in my head that says, calm down if at all possible, this too will become history, and the fellow will grow up one day. In fact, the minute he gets a woman all will change. I looked around the class, wondering if, by examining their bent heads, I would find a thing to write, wondering if indeed those bent heads were this day of my life.

'Now,' she said, after we'd been writing for a half-hour, the noise of pens scraping paper a bit quieter than craftsmen beating patterns on copper, although being the same thing really. In warm countries they do the beating outside and the sound blends with the glory of the heat, tip tapping to the chorus of conversation, probably echoing me and old man Dinkin.

'Let's hear about your days,' she said. Suddenly we were all nervous – she expected us to read it too? That was a bit much. If she'd told us that we might have written different things, put our Sunday Best into our sentences. The teacher left a moment or so dangling there, waiting for a volunteer, but when one didn't materialise, she said, 'All right, I'll choose.' The first, a woman, read about daffodils, of all the things in the world. I could hardly believe my ears. The second, a man, explained to us the gist of what he'd written. He talked about his wife having a baby. She had had a section after twenty hours in labour, he said, with a hint of wonder or weariness. He used the word section, not preceded by Caesarean, showing his familiarity with the procedure. Some of the other men shifted about on their chairs, looking as if they thought he shouldn't be talking about such things.

Then there was a story about a man who was trying hard to fit in. At school he hadn't been liked much, with good reason. His father, an athlete, had either beaten any of the other fathers who ran, or had not picked them for a team when he became a football coach. No, he was not liked. All the pupils had been told to stay away from him. The strain of the memory showed on his face.

The next one interested me most so far. The woman wondered who ever thought of calling a war Great. She wrote about what had been known as a school of drinking women. Her story was set in Australia. I liked that, never having heard drinking put with school. During the Terrible war, after they'd fed the children and done the washing, they gathered in the snug of a pub, to see if anyone had any word of their men. They were never certain if no news was good news. 'I don't even know where he is,' one of them said, and they didn't know if she meant she didn't know his whereabouts or that she did, but the whereabouts was an alien place. The drink helped for a few hours.

I looked out the window for a moment, imagining those women and what the sound of them might have been. I thought if you were swimming in the pool that looks into our library, and your eye landed on us, you'd never guess right what was going on.

Then it was my turn. My neighbour called my name as if I were a stranger, not the man she sometimes did messages for. I stood up to read. I had written about a husband who had left the town where I grew up. He had been missing for some time, although the wife didn't seem as anxious as we thought she should be. She had a way of standing with her hands on her hips and fixing her eyes on a spot too far away for anyone else to see. She spent time, occasionally, trying to make those hips smaller, and she shouldn't have bothered because they were fine as they were. Her bent head made people think she was listening to them, but if they'd looked closer, they'd have seen the escape route marked out in her eyes. She could stay silent in a queue, not having to tell the world her small things.

And then one day her husband came back as a woman. Strode up the street as if it was his own, went in the front door as he had always done, took his hat off and hung it on the peg in the hall. By the time we had realised who that was who had just passed us, by the time we had turned our heads to stare, the door was closed. We kept a close watch on it until he emerged the next morning. In truth we couldn't believe our eyes, and looked out from under our lashes, as if through half-closed curtains, thinking he wouldn't see us staring if we did that instead of looking at him straight on. He was changed, yes, but funny enough still the same. It was the men mostly who tried to get to the other side of the road if they saw him coming.

His wife took him back and did her best to carry on as if nothing had happened. We didn't know what she felt about it and were afraid to ask, but we did remember her lack of anxiety. It taught us a thing or two; if they could get on with it, there was hope for a lot of things. We let the days pass, trying not to think about it too much, occasionally being pleased with our tolerance. Mary O'Leary decided one Monday to loan him her *Woman's Weekly*. We were shocked at this, it seemed to be going a bit too far, but it settled something for us. The husband took the *Woman's Weekly* and the skies didn't fall.

People are great at getting over things, I wrote – long ago towns could move on even after hangings in the square. And yet they can remember well too, sometimes. In the village next to ours no one would buy the house where a woman had been murdered; it was on the market for five years. It made me fond of that place. Eventually a man, a stranger who didn't know the history, came in and made a shop of it, and couldn't understand why no one bought a single thing. It had to have around four changes before anything worked.

I put other people in my story, including a woman I knew who, for six months, had been addicted to Thomas Hardy. Even when she gave him up, she was still jumpy, expecting the worst. I left it at that, and said I might add more later.

My neighbour looked at me oddly, no doubt wondering if it had been a good plan to ask me here, wondering if she'd figured me all wrong.

She got us then to talking about what we had written. I, unexpectedly, thinking of the school of women drinkers, found myself saying that piano tuners got lots of work when the war started. People turned to music, lifted the lids all over the place, sat down and lost themselves in notes put together long ago. Those who knew the difference called in the tuners. I had thought about that a lot when I lived in a house once owned by a man, a musical-instrument maker, who had found refuge in our country, a man who kept his thoughts easily to himself, because he didn't trust his listeners to understand.

With all this talk of things we knew and thought we'd forgotten, the class flew by. And in no time at all weeks too had flown by. Some of it wasn't good for me. I asked my neighbour if I could stop reading from her list because a few of the stories were keeping me awake at night. I told her that she should never have given me 'A Letter to Harvey Milk'. Did she not know that a story like that would make me cry? Wasn't she the one who kept talking about the relevance of art, did she not see …?

'I did,' she said, 'That's why I gave it to you.' I thought about leaving then, but something made me stay, some last-ditch reason to make the things I know rhyme with others. By the time the term was over she had used me often to kick-start her class and for that, she said, I will get messages done any time I need. But I'm not sure if we'll ever be the same, if we can ever again be just neighbours. I saw her talking to old man Dinkin yesterday, who is, after all, an easier-read man than me.

Up at the Library

Monsieur Black, as he was known in his new life in Monaco, woke in his apartment when the first stripe of golden sun cut into the space not covered by the purple drapes. He climbed up out of his dream, rubbed his eyes and turned over to see if he could steal another few minutes' sleep. But that was not necessary: he'd had an early, drink-free night, oh yes, that's right, he had. So he sprang out of the bed, threw the curtains open and casually glanced out at the harbour, in the way of a man who had lived here for more than a year. The yachts were still there, safely moored, bobbing a little, as if they too were shaking themselves from out of the dawn and into the day. Some time since last night a cruise ship had slid in, taking over a large part of the view from out his window.

Beatrice Duffy woke in her apartment in Beausoleil as soon as the sun rose elegantly from the rim of the sea. She took her cup of tea out to the balcony, not wanting to waste one moment of the dazzlement of this, as is the way with visitors who know their time is limited. She was here by the gift of a philanthropic award, offered the chance to dive into the hinted secrets of past literary lives along the Côte d'Azur. She was up at the library every day, trying to include left-out people in the story of the place, or sometimes adding interesting things about those who already hovered in history. She felt every moment of her delight. She could be seen from other balconies touching her heart every now and then, her waking face beaming out to the parts of the ocean she could see between the buildings. Oh look, there was another ship making its way in.

Soon enough, she went inside, dressed herself for the day and made her way out from her Odalys apartment to Boulevard du General Leclerc. She spent a few moments thinking of his military history before letting herself be seduced into contentment by the perfectly warm morning, the smell of the bakery, the chatter of the market outside Palais Josephine. Beatrice spent a lot of time in the past and sometimes had to remind herself to get on up here – today was waiting too. Here she was in Beausoleil, walking on the beaming circles chiselled into the pavements, reflections of faces radiant in the sun. She walked on down Avenue de Monte-Carlo, having passed the casino and the Hôtel de Paris, keeping her eyes trained for the gradual full appearance of the blue sea. The yachts were still there, safely moored, bobbing a little, well into the morning now, with men and women scurrying about them polishing. She would take the bus at the next stop, get to the library and have her day assembled before the hour was out.

Maurice Vale woke in his hotel a stone's throw from Place d'Armes. He pulled back the curtains, glimpsing the settling in of office workers in the high building opposite him. It's possible that sight of the sea could once have been got from this window, maybe even as recently as a year ago, but the absence of it didn't bother Maurice. He hurried out to get himself a seat in the square, under the perfectly glowing sun. He listened vaguely to the excited, well-alive shouts of the market men and women. You could be in a tune, he thought, but then he would, being well buried in song names at the moment.

'*Bonjour, monsieur.*'

'*Café et un croissant.*'

He too was up at the library, cajoling a song collection into shape.

The waiter came back in a flash. '*Bon appétit.*'

Yesterday a visitor to the library had told him the upper classes did not give that greeting. He wondered about that for a moment. Information received when travelling was not always true, but could still be welcome for all that. Maurice opened his book; a few pages would go well with this perfection. He was reading *Why Birds Sing*. He could have missed the sound of a lark above the morning clatter, but there it was. Yes, he could hear it, surely that was a lark, its call rising above the sound of the shouting marketeers. He would walk up the hill and take a look down towards the sea, get a jolt of pleasure before getting down to his task. He took the steps, slowly thinking about what he would do today, then turned at the bend in the road to look down on the beautiful expanse. The yachts were still there, safely moored, bobbing a little, he presumed, although he couldn't be absolutely sure from this distance. He could see a cruise ship and wondered for a moment what a life with little to do would be like.

As he reached the library, he heard the voices of schoolchildren, shouting out in that delighted way they do. The doorbell chimed to his press and in he went. He spent some moments exchanging cheerful morning talk with

Juliette, who had already opened the library day, set it up for its intended events.

Maurice laid out the song sheets again, this time for thematic arrangement, having already placed them in alphabetical order. As soon as he had done that, he peered around the door to see Beatrice, the other Irish scholar, whose eyes by now had dropped into their engaged, distant look. Maurice and she had crossed collegial paths before in Dublin, but here they were keeping a certain distance so far; they knew how to be strangers, acknowledging each other's climb up the word count of what it was they had set themselves for this week. And when that began to be achieved, they would know by unspoken signs when to loosen their privacies.

'Good morning.'

'Good morning. Nice walk in?'

'Lovely. Beautiful day.'

'And what about the sea, and the boats?'

They could have kept going with superlatives, marvelled all day about the surroundings, but they stopped themselves. They had work to do, thoughts to organise, words to be put together, meanings to be said, so that others could add them to what they knew. There was always more to be learned.

'Where are you at now?' Beatrice asked.

'I'm at another beginning I'm afraid. But I know what it is, so that's something I suppose. What about yourself?'

'I'm listing the writers who came and their dates, imagining who might have met whom. I'm trying to figure out the times after the wars, who came then. And getting a picture of the terrible things they had to set about forgetting. Really I want to imagine that the Fitzgeralds crossed with the Kellys in America, but that's another day's work.'

They smiled at each other, both knowing where days like those could end up. Beatrice had read Frank O'Connor's 'Guests of the Nation' when she was thirteen, and so had found out that life was not as uncomplicated as everyone had pretended so far.

'Great, better get on with it then.'

And they both set about doing just that. Beatrice took up her pen to start something. She had a plan to put order on her long essay, if that is what it was. She had a secure publishing place for it, which gave her free rein to let her mind tinker. She had already made her way to the Hôtel du Cap-Eden-Roc in Antibes. She had needed to see the sweep of the beach, the rug that it had created for all the fun. From the street she thought it looked like a bruiser of a building, well fit to house the endless luxuries that had taken place within. She didn't take the tour, but waited under the palms, looked out to the sea, walked back to Juan-les-Pins humming, 'Where do you go to, my lovely, when you're alone in your bed?' The song fitted sweetly.

When the sun began to settle, she made her way inside. She bought a long beer and listened as the people at the next table talked about their tour, what they'd heard of the writers' lives and what it put them in mind of. They were interested in the stardom of it, the parties. These were not the main things that Beatrice cared about, but they added serious frivolity to her facts, rounding them into more honest realities. She twisted a bit of her brown hair around her ear, bit her lip and thought she should check if Sartre, de Beauvoir or Camus were nearby when Scott and Zelda were here. Scott and Zelda before dissolution. And probably for that reason she suddenly remembered her own given-up marriage, in her left-behind past. In the end it had faded out with as much tight lipped civility as could

106

be expected, at least in comparison to some.

She remembered the evening it was over; they were on a short holiday. The sun was dropping, streaking the sky with colours. Silence was gathering itself together.

'See you later,' they heard a woman shout as she closed the gate, the sound carrying up the silent hill. Even without 'love' being added, the light skip in the words pierced Beatrice right through. Some days she was full of longing.

'We could go down and see the neighbours,' her husband said, knowing what she was thinking, having a terrible fear that this house was going to close around their throats and choke them. There was no possibility at all of driving anywhere – even the most foolhardy would not attempt that hill after dark.

'What neighbours? Surely no one lives here after September?'

They could both feel the melancholy drown them. But that had been then, this was now, she would not sink into that hole again. She brought herself back to the present. She made her way, at a pleasant pace, back to Beausoleil. Who could not love the address.

On the Thursday morning, as Beatrice crossed the road by the school, she realised, with satisfied delight, that it was only her fourth day; as the sun had gone yellow over the sea this morning it had seemed like her seventh. The thin lift brought her to the library door, the bell sounded out among the books, she entered. '*Bonjour*,' she called cheerfully.

'Good morning,' Juliette replied. She waved, lifting her eyes for a moment from her task. She was hand-stitching the next library programme, delicately sewing it with silk thread. It looked like a dusk task, a job to be done as the birds came in to roost, a job that would give any passer-by puzzled pleasure.

Maurice straightened his yellow tie before reaching out to pick up the next bundle of songs. He had got as far as 'I' yesterday: 'I'll take you home again, Kathleen'. He glanced at the names, trying not to get distracted by what some of them brought to mind. At lunchtime he must go out to the winding streets of the old town, down to the shop near the palace. He had people to buy gifts for and they bought back for him – he tugged at his tie again. He placed the packets he had already sorted on the table below the picture of Grace Kelly. During the working day that was her name, the keeper of these rooms. The evening events returned Princess Grace to her.

Juliette said, 'You know that's where Burgess played the piano,' and handed them invitations to an evening at Madame De Treó's apartment up towards Beausoleil. 'This will get you away from the books and the songs,' she said.

The previous Saturday, Monsieur Black had also been asked by Madame De Treó to come see the Aboriginal painting she had bought for a song before she left Australia with her late husband. He had become late while they were here, enjoying their wealth, but when he died, she'd found that he'd bought a bank in Liechtenstein, one that now had no money in it. And what use was a bank with no money. She had lawyers out looking for where it had gone, but they weren't too hopeful. Still, she had plenty yet, and lots of dreams on her walls. Monsieur Black wasn't sure what constituted a song and suspected it might be more than that to him. Money was a strange thing at her soirées. The inconsequential-looking man beside you could be worth a blinding figure, too ridiculous even to say. Monsieur Black was not in that league, hovered below the first rung of it, but he was accepted in this circle for other reasons and no one knew quite what those reasons were. This place was like that; secrets surrounded people, questions were carefully put. Madame De Treó placed him in the evening.

'Did you get to meet the orchestra?'

He had. That was the thing about here: all sorts of invitations if you made the effort at all.

Then she asked, tentatively, with love in her voice, 'The dancers?'

Yes, he had. 'At the end of the evening, and funny thing, they all smoked. And yet they had the breath for dancing.'

'They're young,' Madame De Treó said, wistfully.

'I suppose. One of them was awfully rude to a waiter. I see no necessity for that no matter how famous a person is. I pulled him up on it, but he told me he was a dancer, had no brains, just feet. I said that it didn't take brains to have manners, but I was on a hiding to nothing.'

A silence seeped out around him.

A man, unknown to Monsieur Black, muttered, 'You said that to a dancer from the Paris Opera who had just performed in *Giselle*?' It was hard to know what tone he was aiming for.

'How kind of you,' Madame De Treó said, hesitating for just a second, before moving to welcome a woman dressed in an azure outfit, made to go with the entire glittering coast, all the way from Hyères to Menton.

Monsieur Black turned away and walked to the back of the room. He shouldn't have mentioned the waiter – who in this room cared about waiters? A woman smiled at him, but got back to her conversation without giving him a second glance.

'Well, I've found out the meaning of nostalgia. I should say what it signifies rather than what it means. *Nostos*, return home, *algia*, longing. Someone is writing a book about the future of nostalgia – I'd like to edit that.' Beatrice laughed.

'There's healthy nostalgia, bittersweet empathy, and then the dangerous one,' Maurice replied.

'So, your songs are bittersweet empathy?'

'They're about longing and loss, I suppose. Trying to remember as best they can. Every singer, every sing-song, would add another layer. I imagine people buying the sheets, taking them home, learning the notes, getting the tune to match the words. It was a time before television: learning your song was vital for keeping the spirit going.'

'Whereas what I'm at is trying to create a pastiche monument with different strands of what people wrote in other times. Maybe it's a riff. And I keep being stunned by how they recovered from wars. Putting behind them became a way of life; I suppose there's no other way. We only learn that after we've lived disaster.'

'You know that in the seventeenth century Swiss doctors believed that nostalgia was a curable disease like the common cold. They thought that opium, leeches and a journey to the Alps would take care of the symptoms.'

Monsieur Black listened. Now that was what he needed. Conversation like this. Who on earth were these people? They did not look like anyone else. He made his way closer to Beatrice but just at that moment she turned her back to him, hurried to the coat stand, picked up her jacket, and slipped out, for all the world as if she was making an escape. Maurice followed her.

Outside the door Beatrice sighed. 'I love that glitz but I don't want to get waylaid. Next thing you'd know I'd be in Jimmy'z at night.'

Maurice didn't know what Jimmy'z was but he would find out. He would like to keep up with Beatrice.

As soon as the door closed a voice was heard. 'They didn't stay long.'

'I know. They're up at the library: she's doing fiction something and he's doing songs something.'

Monsieur Black left soon afterwards. For some reason, the overheard conversation had unsettled him. He had his own problems with nostalgia. From having been a constant enough man in his twenties he had turned into a bit of a rake, a new woman every few years, always younger, and getting incrementally so, putting the cliché on like a well-fitted glove. Friends who still wanted to love him said he was a romantic, in an effort to put a gloss on the fact that, really, he was a philanderer. When he was finally stung by the loss of real love, he took the gloves off and set out to learn to live by himself. That's what he was doing here. And what a place to do it. But last week when waiting for his aperitif companions to arrive he had sat down. He gazed distractedly at the yachts. It was quiet, not much movement of boats, this was not a fishing harbour with the bustle of work shouting its way in and out. There were few people on the decks, mostly workers cleaning, perhaps getting ready for the arrival of owners, perhaps maintaining the glisten for no one at all. And it was then he saw her: a woman dancing on the deck with her young son. He could not hear the music they moved to. He was overcome with sadness for her, even though there may have been no need. Perhaps the sadness was for himself.

He walked down the street steps from Madame De Treó's apartment block. On the flat now, he began his distracted walk home, checking with himself if he had to pass over Boulevard du Jardin Exotique. It was then that he saw Beatrice and Maurice – they must have stopped for a coffee. He was suddenly overcome with the desire to follow them, to hear what they were saying. There was no harm in that. He got into step behind them, and heard bits and pieces of their patterned talk before branching off to go to his own apartment.

The following morning brought a playful sea mist; it rose from the ocean gradually exposing the boats, then the buildings, before descending again but leaving chunks of houses riding on its top, for all the world as if they sat on thin air. Monsieur Black spent the day doing the things that he usually did, but feeling somehow dissatisfied in a way that was not normal for him. It was coming up to half past four when an idea came to him. He would go up to the library and wait to see if he could catch those two. He took a coffee at the street corner cafe and watched the door of the Fondation building. Finally, he saw them come out, Beatrice first, Maurice after, and, without thinking of what it might look like, he meandered over, sidled into their wake and followed as they crossed Avenue de la Quarantaine towards La Condamine. He stayed close enough to hear the coming and going of the conversation.

'So how did you go today?'

'I've come to the point where I'm a bit stuck; you know, when you've forgotten the light that was there when you started.'

'Would a glass of something help?'

'Might do.'

'Will we try the waterfront?'

And they walked all the way down, stopping to look out over the sea. Monsieur Black kept at a discreet distance for this gazing out. When they reached the port Beatrice said, pointing to Le Botticelli, 'I like La Veranda for a beer, but here is good for a glass of wine. So, yes, wine for me.' The waiter came, brought them their drinks. Beatrice held hers momentarily up to the sky. 'Cheers.'

Slainte.

Monsieur Black had taken an empty table and ordered his drink. He faced out, away from them, so they would not notice his face.

'And you? How are you getting on?' Maurice asked.

'Great day today. Well, at least I learned what I cannot use. You see, you could get overwhelmed by all that is said, but really what matters is that you go back to one thing they wrote or made. I'm including Eileen Gray's house. It can be too awful to know how some of them lived. I'm trying to forget the terrible things that happened.'

'In their lives you mean, not just the wars?'

'Well yes, what they did to themselves, each other, and what was done to them too. Oscar Wilde came down here after getting out of prison but it didn't go well. A group of English people recognised him and booed him out of a restaurant.'

'It would have been easy to recognise him, poor man.'

'And the Nazis using Eileen Gray's lovely wall for target practice. You know Burgess used to shout up to Graham Greene's apartment, insults about the lover and all kinds of other slurs. That's more recent of course.'

'As for the Fitzgeralds, it's hard to concentrate on the good times when we know what came after.'

Beatrice was trying to imagine a mark they might have made down on the beach with their dancing feet, one that the tide hadn't washed away with the lives that followed.

'So, tell me about the songs,' she said.

'Here,' Maurice said, and handed her a list. 'There are 1,099 titles. Well, a few are repeated, but not many. I want to put them together in such a way that people can see what things lead to what. Or maybe there are no links at all. That could be good too.'

It took Beatrice a few minutes to look through them.

'Oh dear,' she said, shivering a little in the heat. She could hear the drum of history, and longing; dance music tuning up, love gone right and gone wrong, and the rattle of gates.

Beatrice and Maurice began then to talk of things that Monsieur Black could not understand, references that made no sense to him. They put such enviable store by them, he thought. As they finished their drink a man he recognised walked by, halting briefly at their table.

'Oh, didn't I see you at Madame De Treó's?' he asked Maurice and Beatrice.

Monsieur Black put the menu in front of his face so as not to be seen. He listened to the exchange of greetings and small chit-chat about beauty.

'You should come up and see us,' Beatrice said.

'Thanks, not sure I'm around after today. I've been in the library of course, awful lot of books, was surprised at the number. Would you have read any of them? Many of them?' he corrected himself.

Monsieur Black couldn't hear what Beatrice replied, but he did notice her shifting her body as if with discomfort. If he was asked to go up and see them, he would have a better answer than that.

When the man had bade them farewell Beatrice and Maurice paid their bill, said a cheerful *au revoir, merci*, to the waiter and walked towards Allée des Boulingrins. Monsieur Black finished his drink, paid his bill and set off in the opposite direction. He felt good. It was such a thing to hear these strange two in this place. As he passed their vacated table, he saw a sheet of forgotten paper, picked it up, folded it and put it in his pocket. At Rue Grimaldi he decided to have another beer and peruse it. It was a list of songs – such names!

Biddy Aroon
A summer shower
Down went McGinty
Come back O'Riley
I'm going back to the one I love
Is there any news from Ireland?
Have you seen Maggie Riley?
His nose on the mantlepiece
A bushel of kisses
Alderman Houlihan's Grand Ball
Ask me not what I'm thinking
Can he love me like Kelly can?
Down at Rosie Riley's flat
Fancy Nancy Clancy
Give me a little bit more than you gave O'Reilly
Has sorrow thy young days shaded?
I'll name the boy Denis, or no name at all
My lodging is on the cold ground
O'Brien has gone Hawaiian
O'Reilly went against it
Oh, call it by some better name
Slavery's passed away
The light that lies
Where, oh where, is my Norah?
Never take the horseshoe from the door

It's no wonder they were interested. He read the titles again. And who was this O'Reilly who turned up everywhere?

It is difficult to say when Monsieur Black decided to follow them every day. Perhaps he only intended to do it once and then it became a habit, like any five o'clock walk might. But there he was, each evening, waiting in a different place, waiting to hear what they had to say. He told himself that it wasn't as if he was following the woman; no, he was eavesdropping on culture, yes, that was it. He heard now about Baldwin, Beckett, Brecht, Chatwin, Christie, Colette, as well as Eileen Gray, whose house he knew well. And James Joyce of course.

Monsieur Black knew that Maurice, on his second run through, was now at the letter M and there were a lot of them, all the Macs and the Mcs. He had by now photographed nine pages, and had ninety-nine more to go. He had got a shape in his head, a picture of how the sheets should look, a thread of how the information should be laid out. Monsieur Black knew that Maurice had started giving the librarian a bundle of song names each evening before she began her wind down, preparing to leave the rooms in stately neatness, allowing the books to sink into their shelf space, lean over towards each other perhaps.

Monsieur Black knew that Beatrice had amassed the disparate histories: Chekhov, Dante, Dickens, Dumas and on to Hemingway, Hugo, Huxley, Tennyson, Tolstoi, Wharton, Wilde, Woolf, Yeats, Zola. And not forgetting Katherine Mansfield, Karl Marx – you couldn't leave him out – Nabokov and Nin, Parker, Plath, Pound and Proust, Sackville-West, Sand and Sartre. She had a timeline. She had circles drawn, a Venn diagram of a dance. She did not still have to be so careful, was not in fear she might lose the rhyme or reason of it, she was past that stage.

On the final Wednesday Maurice came out of the library early, to tend to last-minute family things, buy presents that he had forgotten he needed.

Beatrice made her way to Le Botticelli. She bought a glass of wine and watched the sea, trying not to forget it because, with all the time spent catching the hours of what she'd read, that would be easy to do.

She looked up at the man who sat down at the next table, and recognised him, from where she was not sure, but definitely recognised him.

'Hello,' he said.

'Are you following me?' Beatrice asked, and laughed, not knowing why she'd said that.

'Good lord no. What made you think that?'

'Just a joke. I thought I'd seen you before.'

'Well, it is a small place – it's possible. Would you like another glass of wine?' he asked.

Beatrice hesitated and then thought, why not. One glass. They settled themselves and Monsieur Black asked if she had been in Monaco long and if she liked it.

'What do you live on?' Beatrice asked, knowing she shouldn't have.

But he didn't seem to mind. 'Oh, money I made without too much work.'

'Was it a lot of money?'

He was slightly taken aback, but really it was none of his business if she overstepped the mark. She could not know this was a forbidden question. 'It was enough. And what about you?'

'Oh, I don't make money, but I'm doing what I want, so that takes up most of my time. I don't have much left to long for things I can't afford. And really I don't want for much.'

She then explained her essay, her long essay, as best she could.

'But do you think that matters?'

'Oh yes.'

'But really matters?'

She frowned – the last thing she needed was someone talking about the value of things. 'Well yes. When times are good, we can enjoy them and all their trimmings, but when times are bad, we have to search below the enjoyment to try to get something more; meaning maybe, or answers, or hope if we're lucky. I want to know what people did, and wrote, after the wars. Or between the wars. Or before some of the wars. All that fear and loss. And worse still the fear of loss.'

Monsieur Black asked her if she'd like to go for dinner but she said no, because although the conversation had been pleasant enough, she did not think it could hold up for a dinner's length. Monsieur Black was gracious with his disappointment, hoped she'd enjoy the rest of her stay and get done what she wanted. They said goodbye.

The pity was that Monsieur Black would not be able to follow them anymore – she now knew his face. So, he never heard where their work had led them, or how it had finished up.

On Maurice's last morning in the hotel he hurried his clothes into his case and looked forward to home.

On her last morning Beatrice had breakfast on the balcony, watched the water below spread to the end of the sky, heard the waking up around her, and was happy that she now knew this picture. She moved in and out to her balcony, taking deep breaths to catch passing whiffs of the sea. In her bag she stacked notes not yet used, paragraphs not yet decided upon and a large sheet with all the names she'd found. She would have to choose which to use, but not yet, so for this while they would all be together on the one page.

Juliette opened the window of the library on to the old town, letting in the sounds that make up a morning, and without which we would lose our bearings. She checked the music cabinet. She returned books to the shelves from where they had strayed. But she didn't wipe away everything of the two departed scholars, not yet: she would rather let the dust of them fade gracefully.

Monsieur Black went through his diary – he still kept an old-fashioned one. He would have to pick up other things again, now that those two were going home.

Beatrice had said that he could always go up to the library.

To do what?

To read.

Maybe that's what he would do. Perhaps when the autumn arrived, when the pool was emptied and the funfair was set up. But why wait? So, before the day was overcome with heat, he made his way up the hill to see if they'd left anything behind.

As the bus pulled in to the airport Maurice asked, 'So, did the Fitzs know the Kellys?'

'Don't know,' Beatrice laughed. 'I'll have to come back to find out.'

How Things Are With Hannah These Days

Hannah Grogan went out to Australia on the assisted passage in the early nineteen seventies with her spanking new husband. Anyone who had been there on the day they left remembered it well; they had all piled out to the airport to wave them goodbye. There had already been weeks of mentioning, looking towards the day as it progressed along the calendar like a tide coming in. Marcus, one young cousin, was, as usual, even more embarrassed than his sister Tara. He had tried feigning a sick stomach: 'Awful pain there,' he said and he touched a spot that he knew always put a worried look on their mother's face. But recently the doctor had told her that there was not one single thing wrong with him, so he was forced into the back of the car, where he promptly kicked Tara, but she didn't bother kicking back because she was thinking of the new spiral building at Dublin airport. She'd seen the picture of it on the back of a shiny magazine and wondered if they would

120

get a look. She was also trying to remember where that could have been, because certainly her mother didn't buy shiny magazines.

There was great excitement for an hour or so as different family members arrived. Then someone was heard asking 'Has Millie come yet?'

'No, of course not,' came a reply. 'I'm glad it's not her that's going – she'll miss her own funeral that one.'

The cousins switched off at this, realising that the same old things they'd heard every Christmas were going to be repeated here today. But then Hannah and the new husband arrived – they never thought of him as having a name, no need really – and the atmosphere changed. The air seemed to get full: there was a lot of overlapping talk, sentences piled on top of each other like sandwiches.

'Oh, I'll be lonely without her,' Hannah's mother said.

'It's only for a few years,' an aunt hurriedly replied, doing her best to minimise the significance of the event, but secretly glad it wasn't one of hers that was going.

'It's very far, though, very far; worse than America, even the west coast.'

No one replied to that.

Marcus and Tara liked this new talk of faraway places and were prepared to allow that their relatives might know something of interest. They didn't even mind the family caravan wiggling towards departures; they quite liked the whole thing really, until the crying started.

At first it was just sniffles, punctuated by the occasional sob, then it reached a crescendo of full-blown weeping, still low enough for passers-by to politely ignore, but then Aunt Mags let out a wail. It came suddenly, apparently not attached to any previous sound. At that stage of their lives, they were not aware of the fact that she was known as a crier. At funerals people tried to rush her away before she got started, and if they couldn't manage that they put as much distance as possible between themselves and her. The sound stopped people in their tracks; they couldn't avoid snapping their necks in its direction. Tara blushed hot scarlet and then ran to join Marcus, who had, with remarkable speed, got himself well positioned behind a pillar so that no one would know who he was with.

That was the last they'd seen of Hannah, years ago. They had missed her actual departure, being so well hidden behind the pillar, and no matter how their names were shouted out to 'come say goodbye to your cousin', they ignored them, knowing that something bad would probably happen to them for this sullying of the moment of leave-taking.

Tara had heard the odd scrap about Hannah since then but wasn't remotely interested; she had growing up to do. But now here was this strange letter, wielding years of Hannah's life in front of her, as if she'd never gone through those airport gates. Being honest with herself, Tara thought she had enough relatives and didn't need any more, whether newly discovered ones, adopted, black sheep – that sort of thing – or ones resurrected. She had become a satisfied enough young woman with no desire whatsoever to do leave-takings at Dublin airport. But manners demand that you don't drop a letter half read so she stayed with it right up to Hannah's peculiar request that she come visit her. 'My mother and yours said that you just might.'

Hannah and the new husband had first flown to London, where they stayed the night in a hotel. Simon was his name. They had gone for a drink in the bar and met a Welshman who would be going on their ship. He had recently left the priesthood, he told them. He had a Teddy-boy haircut, which had been all the rage when he went into the seminary. He thought, all things considered, that it would be best to start again far away from Carmarthen. Hannah had found something shockingly sad about him, epitomised by the sartorial years that he had missed. She thought she would avoid him on the boat if she could, and immediately felt mean. In the morning, while she was getting ready and checking the bags once again, just to be sure, Simon had gone shopping, got delayed and almost missed the bus to Southampton. God how she remembered it. The panic had made her realise what she had done, and where she was going, and how far away it was. But she couldn't turn back now. She had tried to look at the English countryside from the bus window – it was, after all, different to her own, and in other circumstances could have been the makings of a holiday. Yet she found it made no impression on her at all. It couldn't get in behind her galloping thoughts.

After some hours they arrived and stepped off the bus, down where the port smelled of port. In the hall leading to the ship, passengers began to queue, some in a more organised, hopeful way than others: English, Scots, Swedes, Danes and a miscellaneous few Irish, none of whom Hannah had yet met. They queued all day, eventually swapping with each other to allow an occasional rest on the seats, and when the visas, the health cards, the passports were checked they were given a cabin number, a number for meals – first, second, third sitting – welcomed aboard, and swallowed by the mouth of the boat. It didn't take long once they reached the top of the queue. They made their ways, over the gangplank, to cabins that were deep down in the noise of the engines.

When their wardrobe was unpacked, hung up, and their toiletries placed on shelves, Hannah went wandering. She found the swimming pool on deck, the hairdresser's, a doctor's surgery, shops, a beautician's corner, a musty library and several bars. Only two hours had passed. She went back to the cabin. It was lucky that she and Simon did not know each other long. There was less danger of getting bored because of that, she thought. They had the lifesaving gear put on and laughed over, even photographed, before any safety announcement was made. One more hour.

At the fourth hour their dinner sitting was called. Neither Hannah nor Simon had ever been on any kind of ship before, never mind a Greek liner, so they stepped their way cautiously to the dining room. They made several mistakes before finding it, but were finally guided by the sounds of cutlery and the smell of apple juice. What first struck Hannah was the size of the waiters: small, almost tiny, men, all wearing black trousers and red cummerbunds. She had never before thought of height difference as a marker of nationality, and was aware of the depth of her awful ignorance; not ignorance as in brutishness, ignorance as in simply not knowing, or not having thought of certain facts. But now she would learn. She was a little disturbed that it was the waiters who first caught her eye. Shouldn't marriage have annulled those noticings? Their designated waiter led them to a table to meet their fellow diners, people with whom they would spend every mealtime for the next four weeks.

Hannah included a photograph of this dinner table in her letter to Tara. It seemed an odd thing to do, a confusing clue to what had become her life.

Hannah had, for years, thought the journey of little interest to anyone except to herself, and then only in flashes,

124

like when a particular kind of bell rang in a supermarket – the type that reminded her, with a jolt, of the ship's call to meals – or safety drill announcements. But in this letter, she wrote the details of the voyage matter-of-factly, as if everyone did spend a month at sea sometime during their lives. When she had posted the letter with the photograph in it she was suddenly embarrassed, as one would be when a private thought slips out to become nonsense once spoken. Too late now.

Before Hannah had put the photo in the envelope, she had looked at the co-diners, surprised that she could remember them so well – not at first their names, but their auras. Him who had given a Masonic handshake to the three men when he had dropped in during their first course to tell them that he was on his way to the captain's dinner, but would see them at the next meal. If they responded, he would know; if not, no harm done because that would mean they did not recognise it. When the men discussed this, Hannah wondered if perhaps he didn't just have a nervous way of shaking hands. How would they know for sure? She resolved to try herself but kept forgetting, and then realised that it would not work anyway, her being a woman. He was a healthy-looking sixty, an old man to young Hannah. He was nifty on his feet. His stepson had run off with his son's wife, so he had a temporary view of marriage.

Then there was the thirty-year-old, returning to Australia after a holiday at home in London. He was collecting places to put down. Already. He had travelled far in Asia and could name all the horrors of 'countries like that'. His funnelled gaze threatened to close down the table. And it was hard to fight, because no one else had been to the places he mentioned, so had no knowledge with which to dismiss his assertions. Not yet, determined Hannah. This man, Lindsay was his name – how peculiar to remember, now that she looked at his picture – talked ceaselessly about travels he had done. At first Hannah thought he was merely introducing himself. But each meal brought a new barrage, and they seemed helpless to stop the flow. He was fascinated by himself. He hoisted place names up poles to establish exclusive rights. The Scottish couple next to him, who made up the last of their group, yesed and noed politely and left the table quickly for a swim after breakfast, a lie-down after lunch, a drink after dinner. Hannah learned how to daydream seriously; it reduced the solo story ramblings to a mere irritant. Luckily, she hadn't caught Lindsay's eye properly on the first night, so now she couldn't be drawn in. She became the person who is not quite present. No one was sure what to do with her: crack their fingers in front of her to make her pay attention or ignore her. She could sporadically hear the others' attempts to change the conversation. The edge in their voices strayed out of tune. She could hear them sometimes putting brakes on their words, stopping just short of shouting him down.

While they talked, Hannah changed herself, and everything she knew, in her daydreams – after all, if she was on a ship, going to the end of the earth, a thing that still pulled her up with surprise, then she could change at will, discard old benign ignorances. Simon didn't mind the vagueness caused by this rearranging, as long as she was with him on the bunk. And her seeming absence from conversation allowed him a chance to grow out too.

After a few days at sea, the ship pulled into Las Palmas de Gran Canaria. It would stay for one night and one day, nestle in the dock while workers tidied its loose ends, scurried up and down its sides, patched up weathering paint and generally got it ready for the next part of its seafaring. By eight o'clock most of the passengers were to be seen in the pubs and cafes of the hot streets. Next day they took a tour. Hannah was much confused by a volcanic chasm and much delighted by her first sight of growing bananas. The air was the hottest she had ever experienced, hotter than she could ever have imagined, as if the fire at home was blowing its heat around her face, outside in daylight. There were mixed emotions going back on the ship. There were those who, having put their feet on dry ground, thought that a few days on the ocean was enough. And there were others who now thought of the ship fondly, as a temporary home, and were pleased to be undertaking the next leg. Almost all stood on deck as the ship was piloted out and the sound of horns melted into the hills of La Gomera and El Hierro and wherever else was twinkling out there.

Even after dinner the passengers came out again on deck and watched the lights as thousands of travellers before them had done. It took hours for them to fade. Some people enjoyed that; some headed into the bars earlier than others, made a little sad by the flickering fade into darkness. At breakfast the next morning Lindsay said, 'Those Las Palmians, seedy sort of people, not to be trusted, I wouldn't think.'

'I don't really like that kind of right-wing talk,' Hannah said. After all she had been there too, so was entitled to an opinion.

'Pardon?'

'I don't really like that kind of right-wing talk,' she repeated, word for word.

Simon was amazed. Did she know what right wing meant? Where had she learned it? She usually took her cues from him, asked him to explain any semi-politics that he had, seemed to believe him. He wasn't too worried about whether she took it in or not; her understanding of his views and the reasons for them would probably not be necessary for their lives. 'Pardon?' he said too.

'It's okay. We heard the first time,' Lindsay remarked, and added, 'they resembled a type of Mexican I've met.'

He had her there.

'But of course, that's only my opinion.' He smiled at her.

'Yes, indeed,' said Hannah, as if she said that sort of thing every day.

Simon, the Scots, and the Mason clattered their cutlery together. What on earth had got into her? She herself did not know. Could less than a week at sea have changed her this much?

The Scotswoman said, 'We had a child who died. That's why we're going to Australia. He died in his sleep, but people kept watching us in our town.' Her eyes filled with tears.

Her husband put his hand over one of hers and said, 'Marge' – that was it, Marge – 'Marge, don't upset yourself. We've left all that behind.'

The clattering of the cutlery softened. Lindsay had been firmly put in his place. From then on he came late to meals and jumped up as soon as he had put the last spoon of dessert in his mouth, running off to join more appropriate company, plenty of which he had found once he had looked. Him having lost command, the Mason took over and amused them all well enough with stories of his son and stepson – presumably the humour helped him cope. A wife was never spoken of, and non-mention of such a nature is so definite it is never questioned. Hannah went back to daydreaming, occasionally taking part in the conversation in a general way. She didn't jump out of her shell violently again, and Simon relaxed. Really, he wouldn't have liked too much of that.

The engines drove them expertly. They journeyed unfathomable miles per day. The *Morning Newsletter* informed them thus. And also of the weather prospects, and whatever news the captain thought they should know. The truth is supposed to be told in diaries and logbooks. Hannah doubted that now, because she had seen the sheets that were dropped each morning outside their cabin. Anything could be happening out there; they would never know. The captain translated the world; they had no choice but to believe him.

Soon the sun got so close that the passengers had to buy stronger sunglasses than they had ever thought they would need, so that they could come out on deck without being blinded. There was too little shade and lassitude governed their hours.

Two things happened on the day they crossed the equator. The ceremony of Neptune visiting was performed, and a couple fell asleep in their deckchairs at noon while their baby burned beside them. It was rushed to a freezer but died two days later. At their table no one, not even Lindsay, talked of it, in deference to the Scots. A few nights after the death Hannah was woken from her sleep by a descending blanket of silence. The ship had stopped, engines were switched off. She came down quietly from her top bunk, put on her dressing gown, left the cabin door on the latch and went on deck to see what was happening. A dozen or so people were huddled at one end, and a few more like herself stood at the stair doors. The baby was being buried. Hannah can still hear the sound of the coffin hitting the sea, and although awed by the loneliness at the time, now wouldn't mind being buried in the ocean. She has sometimes wondered since if there really was a coffin and if so, who made it. She has wondered if maybe they were simply having prayers. Back in her cabin she cried quietly, and thought of distance, and how she missed her brothers, and how there was no point any more in being mad at them for anything. They were too far away to feel it. That would leave her some spare time, she thought. And what she wasn't going to do with it!

Mercifully, the days cooled a little as they hurried away from that line of zero degrees, that equator. They ate up a not significantly different number of miles per day. Out there, somewhere beyond the water, a line of land would bring a person into Congo, Angola, Namibia. More days now. And still the captain told them what he would. There were times when torpor knocked Hannah sideways and she collapsed outside on a deckchair, unable to make it back to the cabin. Once she discovered that she had slumped down beside Lindsay. She was too surprised to get up. So was he. He mock saluted from his burned forehead then let his hand drop, too hot to attempt a putdown. She wished she could stand up to him, and wondered if there was a way to get confidence if you weren't born wealthy.

The next stop was Cape Town, and that imminent event caused a little excitement at some tables. It started at the table next to Hannah's. Normally, conversations could not be overheard, but this one was loud. There was a man sitting only feet away, an unnoticeable man who Hannah had not seen before. But now his raised agitated voice drew all eyes in his direction. He was launched into a full-blown, fierce attack on the anti-apartheid movement. And once begun at that table the debate picked up momentum and engulfed a few more.

'How do you think that they'd be able to handle the diamond market.'

'Don't they have to X-ray them in the evenings coming up from the mines in case they have them swallowed?'

'And what on earth could they do with a few stones? Where do they think they could sell them?'

'How do you think that South Africa got rich?'

'Who do you think made that happen?'

'Well, you always have to have some people poorer than others. That's the way things are.'

'Yes, that much poorer, in some instances. It's the only way.'

'What has sport got to do with it?'

'If they were good enough they'd get to play.'

'But they're not allowed.'

'Oh well.'

Towards the dessert the topic was changed because, while there was nothing wrong with an occasional argument over dinner, it was best not to push it too far. Because it could carry on out to the bar. And then what might happen? A bit of a dust-up in a ship's bar could escalate into an almighty fracas. No one wanted to end up cooling their heels down in the brig.

Surprisingly, at Hannah's table, Lindsay did not loudly hand out his pre-prepared view. Perhaps it was because the first murmurings started to heat at their neighbouring table, and even he could see how stridency was not making for great comfort. The Mason was wiser than to open his mouth at all. And the Scots appeared bewildered, although you never could tell what they were thinking, Hannah now knew. She had often been taken by surprise by the last thing they said before they left the table. But they would arrive for the next meal and begin again as if they had not left a parting wonderment behind them. Hannah realised that she had only one meal in which to think out her own view; think it out for herself because, in truth, she had not given the question much thought before. And hadn't really registered that Cape Town would be a docking port for them. But she wanted to come to her conclusion before dinner was over, so that someone else would not be able to tell her what to think. She did know that one ship's dinner was not a long time for the settlement of such an issue.

Later, the conversation between Hannah and Simon centred on whether they should get off and go into the city or not. He thought that yes, they should. 'To witness' was what he said. He said that he had read a lot about the act of bearing witness. Hannah did not know if he had or had not. She wasn't sure if they should get off because some of the others weren't, said that it was breaking sanctions. Also, she had heard some of the choice words being spoken by two men, including the man from her neighbouring table, in the corridor on their way from the dining room. The words had almost winded her and she wasn't sure that she wanted to see what they meant. But, as the ship followed the pilot into the port, and Table Mountain shed its cloth of cloud, and the crew swung out noisily over the sides of the vessel, again to hose and scrape and paint, the urge to put her feet on the ground was too much for her. She would witness.

There were two things to be remembered from that day. The mountain. And in the park, with the squirrels darting about, Simon had held her hand and told her that he would mind her and that she should not worry about politics too much; there was nothing she could do. And, although Hannah hadn't particularly ever thought that she needed to be minded, she did appreciate him saying it, even if it puzzled her. But once they came out of the park, and once her eyes came down from the mountain, the rest was ugly.

Hannah was stunned by the detail of the segregation laws. How had they been worked out to such extremes? What diligence and thought had gone into them. Was there an office just for this alone?

'Like the one in Rome that reads the sermons of priests to check for heresy,' Simon said.

'Stop joking,' Hannah said, and wondered if he was.

All day they walked, and all day she saw and was astonished. She would never forget it. They stopped outside a busy shop where people could rent or buy films. A man, seeing their curiosity, told them there was no television here. It would not be proper to have black people and white people watching the same news, and no one had yet figured out how to segregate it. They could never be sure if this was true, but what they could see, before their eyes, made it likely that it was. Taxis for whites only. Separate public telephones and toilets. The stamp queue in the post office: a line for whites and one for blacks. What on earth for? thought Hannah. What could happen in a stamp queue? She wanted to go into the other one but was convinced by Simon that that would not be a good idea.

'They wouldn't want you to,' he said.

'Which they?'

'Shssh.'

Beaches for whites only. The city, after six, for whites only. At five minutes past six they saw a black man being beaten off the footpath. When he got away from the blows, he ran very fast. They went back on board earlier than they needed to, Hannah saddened beyond her comprehension. And that day did indeed change her.

As the ship was pushed out gradually, parting from the wharf, vibrating noisily as it turned its face out to sea, black men shouted to the passengers on deck, 'It's a great country. Come back.' It was hard to figure out what they were really saying.

At dinner that night there was a peculiar silence. The table that had proved the noisiest before reaching land was now a model of politeness.

'Do you need salt?'

'Are you interested in a game of cards afterwards?'

'Which barber did you go to the last time?'

The politeness drove away the listening ears from other tables. Conversations began to rumble on to an even keel around the room. That night they watched the last land lights they would see for a fortnight, unless they happened to be up in the night and spot Madagascar, or imagine that they did. The rumour was out that they would be able to see it. Others believed this not to be true but couldn't be bothered arguing. Hannah looked out and wondered why she was here, how she had allowed herself to get here. She had forgotten the day she got on the ship, had forgotten her surprise at the swimming pool, and forgotten being first told how it was emptied during rough seas.

'The pool's empty.'

Now she knew this meant that a new storm was gathering, or maybe, luckily, that there had been one during the night and she had slept through it, as the cabin tipped this way and that, and the glasses rattled. Simon had stopped saying, 'It really is like a floating hotel.' There were only so many times one could express a wonder out loud. Hannah had stopped trying to imagine the ship as someone in the sky might see it. She was rooted in it now. She was not surprised anymore at the solidity and the sweep of the staircase, and often took the lift up to dinner. She didn't see the gleaming silver on the table anymore, or the white gloves on the waiters, or the smallness of them.

This worried her. One of the waiters had stopped her in the corridor. She had always smiled at him, thinking him maybe as lonely as she sometimes was. He asked her if she wanted tea in his cabin; he would be off in an hour. She made a choking sound and stuttered out, 'I'm married.'

'I know,' he said.

She was more surprised at having said she was married than at his request. She now blushed furiously every time he came to their table. He sometimes winked, and then the settling that she had arranged on her face would collapse into redness again. He would smile a small victory.

Hannah began to visit the library. It seemed so peculiar that this room had managed to recreate any or every library from her childhood, except the mobile van of course, and maybe even that, she thought, as she perused the shelves. It was the only room that did not at all appear to be at sea. And she hid herself there when she and Simon had reached an unremarked-upon tiredness with each other's company. There she managed to forget the competitions, the guessing how many miles the ship would travel in the night, watching people drop their answers in the glass on the way into meals. Once, she aimlessly wandered into a Zorba The Greek dance class, and she tried some steps. The teacher was enthusiastic, but his voice appeared to have an exhausted tone to it as he made an effort to put the enthusiasm in tandem with his feet. Hannah was embarrassed by her incompetence. It was as if her own way of dancing was such an intricate part of her body that it stopped her from moving in time to Greek music, that it stopped her from straying over into a different rhythm. Surely that couldn't be true. She looked at the others, who had certainly got the hang of it, and wondered if they had been going every day. She preferred the library. Somehow, she could be her own self there. She grew very glad of this sanctuary in this long stretch of water. She still followed the progress of the ship each morning on the noticeboard, but it seemed only to be treading water, not moving along just out of sight of imaginable land. She got tired of the hairdresser's, and couldn't anyway have anything more cut off her hair. And she certainly got tired of watching the tennis players.

One night, which was the same as any other, they sat looking out to the vast distance of nothing, heard the water lap, and talked in seafaring rhythms. Hannah tried to count the days that they had been at sea but could not recall them. They all ran into each other, as if nothing differentiated them, as if her sense of dawn and dusk had been lost. But maybe the water speeding under their ship was a way of being. In the quiet spot that they had found she could hear the ship creaking. Strange birds called out to each other, away out there in the dark. What if some of the passengers got sea madness, the way some people can get snow madness, in Alaska, she supposed? Went mad looking at snow and just drove into it. What if that happened here, if people started jumping over?

'What if you had been forced to do this journey? People were,' she said.

'Oh, don't be thinking about things like that. Let's go to the bar.' Simon was determined to protect Hannah from her own thoughts. At the bar they had a good night, sipping drinks slowly and watching others who were drinking faster.

A voice was heard shouting in the corridor at dawn, 'You can see it, you can see it.' People jumped from their beds and ran out on deck. They stared, stunned by the joy of seeing land, secretly relieved beyond words. How it had come up on them fast in the end.

'We're a full day off yet,' Lindsay said, and they had to hand it to him, he would know.

'Does he mean twelve or twenty-four hours?'

That's as much doubt as they could suggest. So, they had breakfast. They all looked different somehow this morning. There was expectation on their faces. It carried into their walks. They were now prepared to listen to Lindsay; he had, after all, been here before.

And all day people stayed outside on deck. They walked around and took photographs of each other; sat straight backed on chairs, suddenly alert. They confided thoughts that they had about this new place, and dreams that they had. And all day the land got closer. No one could go inside. This getting closer had to be watched. It was too good to be believed.

Small vessels manoeuvred alongside and men in immaculate suits came on board with briefcases in their hands. Hannah felt like touching one of them, putting her hand on someone recently come from land. They were bankers, insurance men, immigration officers. Immigrants getting off at Fremantle for Perth had to have their checks done now. Simon joined a queue to set up a bank account. There was no hurry to do this, them going to Sydney, but it settled the arrival in his head. He thought that there was no need for health insurance, even though Lindsay had warned that there was. He would tell Lindsay that he had got it. And check with someone else later.

The immigration authorities called the immigrants to the cinema. This was a place that Hannah hated. She had tried once to watch a film there, but had felt nauseated and lost as the screen seemed to roll away from her. Now the officials showed them a film, pictures of what their futures should be like. The women wore pink fluffy slippers, had pink fluffy dusters, which they swiped at gleaming front doors, then turned to brush dust off their husbands' collars as the men left for work. Hannah couldn't figure out if this was meant to be real. Chuckles, some nervous, could be heard.

'Not me,' said Hannah.

'Shssh,' Simon said. 'I know, but don't say it out loud.'

Hannah must check if she was right about the meaning of irony. Sometimes a word didn't mean what you had always thought it did.

The ship moved into Fremantle Port. The first streamers were thrown at it. People stood and waved half-heartedly and then frantically when they saw who they knew. Hannah waved too, but not to anyone she knew. She did not feel strange about this. The crew, looking like little mice, scurried over the sides to hose and scrape and paint again. The police arrived to take away the parents of the dead baby for questioning. Some had forgotten about that. Hannah didn't see a coffin being carried off, so maybe it had been a funeral.

Hannah could never remember walking off the ship at Fremantle. Because they were travelling further, it was a false promise, this walking off. But, also, a trial run. And she was half glad to get back on board to consider what the run had been like.

The next couple of days were spent peering for land again, eyes scrunched up, as has been done forever once the outlines of a country have been seen. As they sailed along and deep into the Great Australian Bight, those who knew their physical geography marvelled at how much desert was out there once you walked inland from shore. As they rounded out of the Bight, comparisons were made between Melbourne and Sydney. These would have to be their move because on the next leg there would only be those who were Sydney bound.

Again, the ship came in, this time through Port Phillip Heads for Melbourne. For those landing here this was the real destination. They had been speeding to this moment since pulling out of Fremantle, some of them having already imagined themselves there. There was much shouting and delighted crying. Again, the crew jumped to hose, scrape and paint and again the streamers were swirled out. There was more cheering. Hannah waved again too. She watched the trunks being offloaded, cranes swinging into the hold and burrowing around in there to get the Melbourne ones, then swinging out with them and depositing them to make small mountains at people's feet. The names were then checked by the passengers standing at the foot of the mountains, cases were heaved on to trolleys and wheeled away. Soon that would be the Sydney-goers.

The city itself left little impression on Hannah, not because she didn't register the clock, the trams, the river, the purposefulness, but because her mind was now too far forward into the next place. She couldn't now remember why they had chosen Sydney and not Melbourne. What if that turned out to be a mistake? The sun shone and rain fell, and men in suits put up umbrellas. Here she heard her first proper Australian talk while sitting aimlessly, trying to drink coffee instead of tea, before waiting to reboard. She made sense of the words, but thought them oddly strewn together and galloped up at the end of sentences. She listened more, and thought that perhaps some people also went up in the middle of the sentences.

'It sounds as if they're putting it on.'

'Shssh.'

'Oh look, there's the Welshman we saw in London. Funny we never bumped into him.'

And on again to a quieter boat. There was a silence at tables where people had been. Lindsay was gone too. They had said insincere goodbyes over dinner. He had not suggested that any of them call if they were ever in Melbourne. The Mason was getting off here, but Lindsay did not offer him his address either. There was a meanness about Lindsay's leave-taking, Hannah thought. She noticed too that his voice had no sound change in it. It stayed at the one pitch. Maybe that was why he had aggravated them so much all along, just the timbre of his voice. The Mason clicked his heels together when he said goodbye. He was all smiles and seemed younger than when he had started the journey. He turned back to take a picture of the table before he left and then had the waiter take another of all of them. Simon did the same.

After the last dinner the Scottish woman called Hannah aside. Hannah did not want to have a private, conspiratorial conversation. She did not want to be given advice. But the Scottish woman said only, 'Some people spend their lives out looking for news of private goings-on. The worse the better. Ignore them. That's all I'm saying.'

'Okay,' Hannah said, perplexed.

'Stay away from people with bad news. Some people love only bad news. This is your chance to get away from all that. Take it.'

'Okay,' said Hannah.

The Scottish man said to Simon, 'Good luck.' And shook his hand heartily.

Then they each repaired to their cabins for their last night at sea. Hannah looked again and again at her passport, as if it could tell her something of her future. Simon checked and rechecked their health certificates and references for the same reason.

'We're in' came the shout at dawn, followed by the clatter of people up the stairs. And they made their way on deck again, where Hannah watched the impossible beauty, dumbfounded.

'Jesus' was all she could say.

She would be happy here, how could anyone not be, she thought, not knowing yet that sometimes more than beauty is needed to pacify a person. And that indeed bad things happened here too. Hannah couldn't have believed this, on that morning.

The ship was now in the heart of the city. Right inside it. Within touching distance of the skyscrapers. The bridge perched and hovered over them to their right. The water shimmered and waved out below the ferries. The dawn, just broken, lit up the entire world. Hannah could feel a lump moving up her throat. Jesus Christ. Everyone on deck seemed to be mesmerised, as if looking at a strange comet, a star just found in the galaxy.

It was then that Hannah saw again the streamers, and the people waving. She did not wave this time, having thought that her Fremantle and Melbourne response might not be the right thing, now that she really was getting off. No one here knew her and it might have seemed foolish, as if she was pretending that there was someone to meet them.

Immigration was speedily got through, because most of the paperwork had already been completed since leaving Fremantle. There were no more questions to be asked or answered. They looked down at their feet as they walked off. Clusters of people gathered around the last luggage mounds and waited for friends or relatives to come back with the car. Hannah and Simon did not have to wait for anyone and a bus whisked them to a hostel in Burwood, where they slept in a steady bed, and the only noise that woke them in the night was the missing hum of the ship.

The following morning they trooped, like people who had been at sea, and lined up to help themselves to a self-service breakfast. They now made the acquaintance of the other Irish who had been on board, having somehow managed not to meet properly while travelling. Darina, from Dalkey she said, told the Greeks, and anyone else within earshot, that there was indeed a difference between her and her husband Paul's Dublin accent. Could they not notice it? She would like her husband to learn tennis here. Hannah moved away as fast as she could. Imagine Darina holding on to that pettiness all the way here. The employers came. They listed jobs for men. They had four building jobs. There were no takers.

'Are there no Irish here?'

The Irish moved their feet and coughed together. The employers left, with the labouring jobs unfilled.

Hannah and Simon ventured out to the street. It was a long road with a hill on either end of it, lined on each side by verandaed buildings. They went to the newsagents under the railway bridge and bought a paper that would get them their own jobs. Hannah would have to learn to type. And she did, sufficiently well in one week, and got her job three days after Simon got his. On her second Friday she was paid, again. She was taken aback, having thought that the first week's pay was for the month.

And thus began a new chapter in Hannah's life. Or her life really, the rest was before and added up to nothing but time

142

and memory. It was the most important part of her life, but it had nothing now to do with her, except to be the past. She walked her new street, down by the Freemason's Hotel, under the railway bridge, to her new job. It wasn't long before she stopped staring, mesmerised, at the verandas, and soon she forgot her own ship's Mason. She did still stare at men in shorts, although she tried to hide this. She found it difficult to believe that a pair of shorts with long socks was considered to be the same as trousers. To her the men looked like old schoolboys. The women wore halternecks on the street and she often watched the outline of their breasts through the flimsy tops. But it was odd how the dictates of heat took the boldness out of clothes. She still wore blouses with collars but was intending to get a halterneck for the weekends.

She did too, and wore it to her first barbecue. The men stayed in one corner and the women in the other, although thankfully Simon drifted between the two, not being quite able to grasp rules that were unspoken. Hannah had to think of things to say to the other women. She could ask what friendship rings meant, and query other things as they came up. Before the next barbecue she'd need to think of better questions. But she knew that she must add something herself. And yet, what could she add? It seemed pointless to speak of home. Empty spaces grew between her and the women. She drank faster. It was better at work where there was a job to be done, and words could be spoken around that, and the words led into conversations. The effort of making new talk began to clear whatever cobwebs of childhood she had left, the child in herself dying with them. This did not make her sad, merely new.

By the time Hannah and Simon moved from Burwood to Stanmore – Petersham train stop, don't miss it – she had the many new things under control and was thinking about what to do with the newness in herself. She got another job in Marrickville, where the Greek women in black greeted her each morning as if she was one of their own. She had never felt European before. She worked in an 'optometrist's', not 'optician's', where the young Greek men came to plead bad eyesight, so that they would not be conscripted to Vietnam. All this distance from sparkling islands to be sent to war. They did not conceive of a machine that could search out their good sight as they sat in the darkened room with the optometrist. She watched them leave, downcast, without a prescription for new spectacles. But they might try something else. Someone might know some other way. They had just got their naturalisation papers; maybe they should have waited until this war was over. Maybe they should have continued tending olives until this war was over. An election drew near and young men hoped. At the beginning of the talk Simon said that he wasn't interested. But as the days went by and the men at his work talked their politics, he got drawn in. Hannah looked at the posters on her way to work. IT'S TIME they declared and it seemed to promise something.

'It's hope,' her boss said.

Hannah could not remember such excitement ever over elections at home. Or maybe it was the strangeness of the canvassing that interested her. Towards the end, vicious words were said about the wives: one described in finery, one in clothes from Bullen Brothers' Circus. It was those words that made her look again at their pictures. She knew which face she trusted most. You can tell a lot from pictures, she thought, even if you cannot hear the person speak. When canvassers called to their door, she wished she could be a full part of what excited them. The big difference in the election platforms was that one promised to put a stop to the sending out of soldiers to a war that was as vicious and as pointless and as unjust as they come. The other didn't. Simon and Hannah went to bed early enough on the night of the count but in other houses, places where it mattered more, the people had parties and stayed up for the first speech, during which, to the astonishment of most, Gough Whitlam, the new man, put a gold frame around several of his promises.

On the Monday morning, with conscription ended, Hannah arrived at work to a long line of young men who had already formed a queue outside the optometrist's. They were there to cancel appointments and to smile. This beam had not been seen in Marrickville since call-ups had fallen through their letter boxes.

In her own street, more Lebanese than Greek, Hannah talked to the young children in the evenings. They were wild, and verbally ruthless, having discovered that their knowledge of English, and their parents' ignorance of it, gave them the upper hand. They could say what they liked – their parents could only look puzzled, knowing that something was wrong, but not sure enough to reprimand. The children were often cruel, knowing that the adults had no way into the nuances of their secret code. The end house had been rented to an Aboriginal family, one that grew and shrank and grew again to a time all of its own. Hannah watched them in the same way that she watched the Lebanese and the Italians, full of delight at their different habits. The Italian men sat in their cars when their houses got noisy; the Aborigines sat in their cars and made them noisy. The Russians, two doors up, twenty years here, spoke of Siberia in serious voices that rolled out fear in front of her.

'Australia is good,' they said together. 'Australia is very good.'

They said it as if it was a warning. When she got sick, they came to the bottom of her bed with a vile concoction, consisting mainly of Galliano and tea, and they sat there until she had drunk it all, no matter how many times she said, 'Later, later.' It did make her better.

The art of being sick away from home helped her further in the making up of a new self. Not that she considered she had to, not that she considered her childhood to have been fractured, having been used to no other. Still, the chance to build outside, in a new light, gave an excited feel to every ordinary day. Simon too began to jump his own fences. There had been no wasted loving while he had been growing up; a little excitement once, when his father had won a teddy bear for the baby at a bazaar, but that's about as far as it went. Simon thought that there had to be more to it than that to create such talk, but he wasn't sure what the more was, and was unlikely now to write to ask. Hannah was, in fact, fascinated by such a minimalist childhood. He used his new days to put things back into his memory, things that had never been there before and that may not have happened at all. It appeared that they were running forward together.

They threw a party, tracking down as many of the people who had been on the boat as they could. Hannah asked two women from work; Simon invited one man from his. And they brought others. This should have balanced the sides of the room. But it didn't work. A conversation blew up about this mixed neighbourhood; words were thrown about carelessly, about *wogs* who kept their shops open all hours of the day. For some reason this late-night hard working seemed to cause particular offence. Hannah flinched at the viciousness of the word; was winded again, as she had been in the corridor of the ship when she had first heard the sound of racism. Old hands at this putdown game tried to get new hands on board. Some turned their backs. Hannah's apprenticeship to the reaches of race hatred, first reluctantly begun on the ship, was being supplemented. She was shocked at such vehemence. But she did not yet know how to change a conversation once it had started. The listeners divided on their reactions but, trouble was, Hannah could not remember who had said what. She liked saying goodbye at the end of the evening. In future she would go to other people's parties. Too much could go wrong at one of her own, she felt.

Her dreams at night became strangely vague. This was better. In the first month she had dreamed often of frost: crisp, dry, white, noisy frost. It was disturbing always to waken into a blinding blue day. On Saturday mornings she let the joyful clattering of Italian men, arriving to help fix up some house on the street, seep slowly into her room. She relaxed into the difference of the strange sounds before she opened her eyes. She could be anywhere. She was anywhere, on her street. She did worry about how dependent she and Simon were becoming on each other for agreed references. This is not how she had thought it would be. She knew that every evening she was telling him things that he did not need to know. She would have to bridge the emptiness that was still there between her and the women she met at barbecues. But she didn't know how, as yet, and worried some more about that.

But still there was enough novelty to fill her time. To last a lifetime she thought. There were countless sounds and sights of extraordinary birds. She would never be able to remember which was which. But she got to know some –

the white cockatoo that flew to her back door on Saturdays and Sundays and chirped up at her, matching whatever Hannah felt that morning. There were parrots and lorikeets. And the more used she became to picking those out, the more she realised how many others there were: strange little birds, hiding behind the big galahs, birds with their own mind-boggling plumage and titillating chirps. She could never tell which one was making which sound. She would have to get a book, of course. That would help with the look of them, if not the sound. Yes, she would start with the birds, before moving on to the animals. It would be good to be knowledgeable about one species.

There were also new manners to be learned. And how not to complain about a single thing. Hannah had noticed that the expression of even the smallest grievance could rouse the mantra, 'Well, what brought you here then?' Once learned, these subtleties helped the flow of talk. The women she ate burnt sausages with were not interested in differences between her and them. Why would they be? They had not chosen to make difference a major, even a minor, part of their lives. She learned that there was no point to comparisons when she was the only person who knew the other. She trained herself out of making them.

On her street there was no sign of the harbour, and sometimes, longing to check its existence, she would take the train for Circular Quay, get on a ferry and pick a stop at which to get off. She tried different views of the bridge and stared transfixed at the sun making stars on the Opera House. She sometimes persuaded Simon to come with her, although he had now acquired some friends who took up some of his time with men's things. Also, she had caught him reading on the last ferry ride. How could he possibly do that? She felt like fighting with him. It was best to avoid that, so maybe she should keep these sallies for herself. If she heard that there was a big ship in, she went down to Circular Quay, to relive a moment of her own. Other people might be standing beside her who did not appear to be meeting passengers. Were they too going back to try to piece together what they had felt on their first day, and to check if they had in fact done all right? Sometimes she hurried away, a little frightened at what she had just remembered.

It was the new friends of Simon's who suggested that they go camping to the bush, and the women could come too. Hannah had not, of course, ever been camping before, and the toilet arrangements might have proven difficult. But, again, the newness of sound and sight, the smell of heat, eased all that. The journey there had had its bad moments. They had stopped at a hotel for a break; the women sipped cold beers and eased the heat from themselves as best they could. After some time, Hannah said, 'Are the men still in the toilets?'

'No, they'll be drinking at the bar. We wouldn't be allowed there. They sent the drinks out here to us when you were at the toilet.'

She felt humiliated by such exclusion – one that hadn't even required an explanation. Perhaps it was the same at home but she'd not known? But later at the campfire, learning diligently the fire-safety rules, and unpacking the food that they'd brought, and smelling the mixed aromas of the cooking, she forgot about it.

Back in the city, as Hannah prepared for some more future that hadn't quite become clear yet, she ordered toasted corned beef sandwiches from the milk bar, without thinking, what a strange way to eat corned beef. She did write home about prawns, and prawn fishing, and rabbit shooting – which she had been coerced into trying, unsuccessfully, on another bush weekend – about long distances, and amusing small peculiarities. But then she grew careful in her letters, trying not to sound as if her life was as different to theirs as it was, trying not to pile up clichés into small mounds of things on the page, getting defensive in the face of the raised eyebrows that she could see, even as she wrote. Soon she might have nothing to say.

From the start, Hannah was not sure that this would be a good way to live continuously, but, for now, was happy. She could feel herself getting interested in the names of places.

Simon began to buy maps.

'Where were you?'

'Buying a map.'

On Saturdays, when they went to the city together, Hannah might turn, feeling him dropping behind. She might see him disappear into a shop. He might turn to look at her, smile, and say, 'With you in a minute.' She might mouth, 'Okay. I'll just go and look over here.'

'There's a place here called Pinchgut.'

'Here?'

'Yes, Australia. I've just seen it.'

He brought maps home from work. Either they had lots of them at his office or he stopped on his way and bought them. He examined them. What was he looking at? Place names? The slant of mountains? The routes of rivers? Where the roads were? It was no wonder that it was he, and not she, who planned their weekends away. And when they would stop to stretch their legs, or have the tea from the flask, there would always be something to see, where mostly there was nothing apparent. He would have known. He was ahead of her.

Hannah did put her feet up on the dashboard. She tried it first to prove that it was only something they did in films but discovered that, done sporadically, it eased the discomfort that long car journeys brought to her legs. She rarely drove on these jaunts. There would be no point. Simon might miss what it was they were supposed to see because he might have put his feet up and forgotten. It was better for him to be at the wheel, and making decisions. He cared more. Sometimes she took up the strip map and checked the information, but by the time she had absorbed it they would be on to the next page. Also, she wasn't sure what she was supposed to be looking for.

It was on one of these weekends that they went to Yass. They stopped at the hotel. Simon had a beer, Hannah tea. She would have liked a beer, but wouldn't have liked to have stopped after one, might have liked to stay in the created camaraderie that drink caused, might have liked not to get into the car again. Because of the beer, it was she who was driving when they came to the Dog on the Tucker Box, nine miles from Gundagai.

'Pull in,' Simon said. 'I've heard of this.'

She was weary already of what might be there. But they did get out and walked about and stared and wondered and got sad about the poor dog, and its master.

'It's only a story,' Simon said.

But Hannah wasn't listening. There was something else here, other than the dog. A wave of loneliness washed over her. She shivered and pulled in air, as if she wasn't able to catch her breath, as if it might run away on her, like a tiny cloud.

'Let's go,' she said, even though Simon hated her saying that, and had told her so. (He said that it wasn't a major aggravation but he just didn't like it.) They got into the car again, and as she pulled away, she checked the mirror, almost as if she was afraid that the place might follow her. She was quiet on the way back to Yass.

'Why don't we stay here?' Simon said. 'Seems as good a place as any. Not much to see, but I don't think there's much else further on either.'

He was looking at the map, searching.

It was a hot evening, hotter even than it should have been. The buildings on the main street looked haggard. Hannah stared, trying to keep the outlines from disappearing into the sun.

'Here,' Simon said, 'here's the hotel. You're not looking.'

She pulled in, parked; they made their way inside. The room was fine: clean sheets, dusted knick-knacks thrown carelessly about to make the visitor feel trusted with domestic inclusion.

'What's wrong with you?' Simon asked. 'You look funny.'

'Nothing,' Hannah said. But that wasn't quite true. A kind of fierce melancholy had descended on her since stepping out of the car in Gundagai.

Downstairs, the bar turned out to be more comfortable than expected. And the first drink made it more cosy still. They could eat here too, in an hour or so.

'Are you all right? You seem distracted.'

At weekends, Simon could be observant.

'No, I'm fine. Fine.'

The evening, surprisingly, turned into a good one; a slow, well-fed stopgap that climbed over the hump of Hannah's dissatisfaction. But in the morning, she was overcome with another sense of displacement. She slipped out of bed and went for a short walk; she would let Simon sleep on, no need for both of them to be miserable. She felt weak with hunger and stopped to hold on to the post of an imposing veranda. Her stomach felt empty. There was a story at home that if you stepped over an unmarked famine grave you would be struck with a ravenous feeling. And here it was, her own personal hungry grass. When she saw the church, she decided to sit there for a moment in its dark, simple coolness. Each long window had two square panes opening out to the sun, the staunch gum trees undressing their barks, and the bleached, thirsty ground. The yellow and red of the stained glass cheered her up. She felt better, but would still be happy to have breakfast and quit this town for the city. Back in their suburb, she wanted to have the order that Mondays brought.

One evening Hannah came home to find that Simon had pasted maps all over the kitchen wall. In a peculiar way she found them comforting. They told her where she was and what was beyond.

'But not the bedroom,' she said.

'Hadn't thought so,' Simon said, smiling.

As if the papering had concluded a search, Simon then began to collect scraps of little-known facts about Australia. He cut them out of newspapers and magazines, copied them from books, and left them hanging about. Hannah could pick them up, smile, and sometimes laugh out loud, then forget them. Which was good, because each time she could smile again, not having remembered.

It was the New Zealanders who invented pavlova. The chef at the Esplanade Hotel in Perth – Bert Sachse, if you want to know, Simon had handwritten in – only perfected it. And named it after a visiting Russian ballerina. Granny Smith apples came into being when Maria Smith threw some Tasmanian apple cores into her Sydney garden. Hannah wondered if these facts were for conversation pieces, or were they to make Simon feel as if he belonged, as if he had known these things all along. She could use them at barbecues.

What did Hannah collect? Nothing much. Memories maybe. And packed them away. She spent most of her time doing a lot of secret planning. In time, this planning ebbed towards a picture of Simon and her going back to Ireland. She didn't want to rush it because she wanted to allow herself to see what had to be seen; it wasn't as if she would ever be back, what with the other things that were in the future.

Gradually, overland maps began to appear on the wall. They would arrive there after some long night's conversation. And Hannah began to drop into travel shops that specialised in overland bus trips. Simon wasn't sure if he had an interest in this sort of thing – surely a plane would be better – but Hannah was adamant. They should return by land, having come by sea. A ship on wheels, over the Khyber Pass, over the Hindu Kush mountains. They would start by flying to Singapore, then Bangkok.

'Okay then,' Simon said. 'We could visit the bridge over the River Kwai, the Australian war grave there.'

'Why?'

'Fellows at work tell me it's an experience.'

'But that's because they have relatives there.'

'It won't take long.'

'Okay.'

And a flight to Nepal, over the mountains and down into the valley. They had recently seen a film set in the foothills of the Himalayas. Hannah could see the joining up of films. After some days there they would board the bus from Nepal to London. India, and definitely Kashmir, Pakistan, Afghanistan, Iran.

'It will be such an opportunity to see those countries. They may not always be open; you never know what's going to happen. And I'll see if I can get us a tour that gives us a few weeks in the Soviet Union.'

'Oh, why not,' Simon said, and Hannah did not notice the hint of incredulity. She would check. She had found one particular agent whom she liked – she asked her.

'Yes, it's possible to go via the Soviet Union. Not everyone wants to do that, so the add-on fare is more reasonable than you'd expect.'

'So, where could we go?'

'Oh, anywhere, as long as it is agreed first. What about this? After Greece turn into Bulgaria and Romania, then you could stay in Odessa and Kiev on the way up to Moscow. You have to be careful what you take into the Soviet Union – they'll confiscate Solzhenitsyn I'm told. Never read him myself, don't know what the fuss is about, is it about sex do you know?'

Hannah said that she didn't think that was the problem.

'Oh well. Then you can go up to St Petersburg,' – the travel agent tracked her pen up the shiny map – 'across Poland, East Germany.'

'And Berlin? Could we stop in Berlin?'

'Of course,' the agent said. 'If you've done that much it would be a pity to miss Berlin, East and West.'

'Great,' Hannah said, 'it's taking shape.'

'It's a good thing to take gum for presents.'

'Gum?'

'Yes, chewing gum. So they tell me. And jeans for Russia. And pens for India. They tell me these things when they come back. Never sure whether to believe them or not.'

'Why don't you go yourself sometime?' Hannah asked.

'Oh, I wouldn't do that. There's no air-conditioning on the buses and no water to drink. You should see the state of people when they come off them.'

Hannah looked at her.

'Only joking, only joking,' the agent said, suddenly remembering that she was supposed to be selling this package. 'I'm going next year.'

At work, Simon voiced his concern about the length of the trip, the journey; more a journey than a trip, which somehow sounded less arduous. He also worried about diseases. It didn't feel disloyal to Hannah, more the natural questions that were needed for preparation.

'Some people now do what they call plane hopping. They stop at four or five places and stay up to three days in each,' Simon said, sounding it out for reaction.

But then Hannah pasted a new, large, complete map of Asia on the wall. There was a red line staggering across it, with x marks at some spots, and occasional blanks. The blanks, she explained, were for the possible detours off the road, and also to facilitate last-minute changes that they might negotiate with the travel agent. Perhaps to see the pink buildings in Jaipur? How on earth did she know about that? There was no more talk about plane hopping. Within days of the purchase of the map, Hannah began to collect other snippets. She brought travel books home, copied out things she thought important by hand and piled them up, where once there had been trivia about Australia. Now Simon could pick up bits and pieces about the Taj Mahal and smile. Wouldn't that be something.

Hannah would organise a farewell party. She would make a list of people to whom they had to say goodbye. And strike off those they could do without seeing. She would begin to track down the people from the ship, any of them that were still here and that she could find. She would begin with Darina. She had not seen them all together since the first months here. It would be a different party, time here having changed them more than the same time at home would have.

The trawl netted news. Des and Anne were separated. Amazing that, how quickly one could learn. They wondered if it would have happened had they stayed at home. Delores and Anne did not speak to each other at all – a serious falling out that had briefly involved the police, terribly hush-hush still, and all the more interesting for that. Brian and Dymphna had come clean about the age of their son. He was not now born prematurely, two months after their arrival. It was a relief for everyone. It had been difficult to pretend to accept the notion of prematurity given the rude good health of the baby before their very eyes. They didn't now give a hoot about what people in Ireland thought – they could go wallow in it, they were never setting foot back there, not even for a holiday, or a funeral.

Hannah did a secret visit to the hostel where Simon and she had spent their first week. It was already changed, buildings having been added on, although the same galah was still making a background noise. She was sure it was the same one. She had been so proud of knowing that new name, never realising that there were dozens more to be learned. She peeped through the window of what had been their room. When they had been in it for a few weeks the previous tenants had visited them. The gesture was sentimental but practical. They came to say that they were now leaving their flat, moving on, and that Simon and Hannah could have it, if they were interested. In turn when they were leaving that flat, they had done the same thing. Gone back to room twenty-seven and offered it to the people staying there, newly arrived like they had been. She wondered if the visit had been kept up, to become a history attached to room twenty-seven.

The Burwood street had not changed: the same incline, of course; milk bars dotted under fluorescent lights; the park, where they had taken pictures of each other, as if it was a perfect setting, not having yet got as far as Bondi or Manly. The Freemason's Hotel still lorded it over the corner. The thin shop under the station, with the *Sydney Morning Herald* sign, still sold papers, but the proprietor had changed and seemed to favour top-shelf magazines more than his predecessor had. She climbed the stairs to the station platform and looked up and down the track. She was surprised, and a little shocked, at how she remembered every single thing. Because of its newness, everything had been noticed and kept, like baubles. Waiting at stations had been a big part of their lives in the beginning. They never minded, having plenty of time. They had used the train a lot at weekends – it had got them out of their flat, where nothing happened and no one called. So far. Like all new immigrants of all times and places, they needed each other, were even a little afraid without each other. They lopped the fears off by standing close. She went back down to the street, not sure if it was a good thing to have looked at the tracks. There was already enough shakiness going on. The decision to go back made it hard to avoid trying to get her life right in her head, and surely that could be a dangerous thing. She left the station.

Hannah would get those paper plates. By the night of the party she would have all her own proper plates packed and away in the crate, not to be opened until they arrived in Ireland. She sometimes shivered with excitement. She would have to buy new clothes, of course, for the overland journey; things she'd get little wear out of afterwards. And she'd have to go to the clinic, talk to the doctor there. The travel agent said that it might be best to take the pill the whole way through the three months; avoid having periods.

'Athletes do it,' she said.

'Really!'

'And the East Germans deliberately got pregnant and then had abortions just before the Olympics. The hormonal change helped them to compete better. The runners and the swimmers and the discus throwers too, I think.'

'I find that hard to believe,' Hannah said, her antennae made uncomfortable by the assertion.

'No, it's true,' the agent said, as if saying so made it so.

'We're going through East Germany.'

'Oh, well, yes. But the Olympics thing isn't really a good example of the place.'

She could spin on a pin. Hannah thought about asking her to the party, but then realised that it was now pointless to be involved with any new people. Now was the time to tidy back and look forward. Indeed, now that it was arranged, she wasn't even sure if there was a point to the party. Still, it might help them to kick this life out from under themselves.

In the end there was no going-away party.

'Still haven't had it, all these years later,' Hannah wrote in the letter.

Simon's accident was such an Australian event. Laughable really, at least in the beginning, before it had gone on too long. It happened early in the week before the party was to be held. He had been driving round a corner that showed one of those sudden wide breathtaking views, the sort that had become common to him, but that were now reasserting themselves on a daily basis, getting him ready for missing them. He pulled over to take a while to look, and wonder what going home would do to them. He was afraid that it might make them empty. It was while he was standing there,

159

lost in thought, that a car sped past. He turned to frown at it – the driver was certainly exceeding the speed limit. As he did so, a surfboard on the roof rack loosened itself, got picked up by a perfect blast of wind, and hit him right on the head. If the driver saw what happened he ignored it and hurried on. When they telephoned Hannah to tell her that Simon was in the hospital, she remained calm. Of course he would be fine – all that was required was her presence and his will. She got a taxi to the Accident and Emergency, asked the driver to please hurry up; he was so slow, she thought. She would try not to cry at him. At the hospital she ignored what the doctors said; would they ever be finished so she could see Simon. And he lay there, looking peacefully asleep. In a few days all will be well, she thought.

As the seriousness of the situation gradually made itself obvious, the few visitors occasionally bristled at Hannah's bright view. 'Away with the fairies,' one of them said. It was clear that Simon was very ill, but even the coma was a surmountable obstacle to Hannah.

'As soon as he's out of the coma, back to himself …'

No one dared say, what if …

Hannah sensed their gloomy predictions, could hear them telling friends later, and hated them.

'Would one of you cancel the party for the minute?'

No need, everyone had heard. It was even on the news. It really was such an Australian kind of accident. Gradually, most of the visitors stopped coming to the hospital. Some occasionally dropped in, but couldn't decide whether they wanted to meet Hannah so she'd know that they did think of her in this the loneliest of vigils, or miss her by a minute, and so avoid that heartbreaking cheerfulness of hers. The best was to meet her at the main door, as she came in and they went out.

Hannah's days became ordered, dreamlike. She collected the deposit on the overland trip, 'It will have to wait until my husband is better.'

The travel agent was so shocked she paid up immediately, not even checking to see if the cancellation insurance had been put through. Nothing like this had ever happened to her. All the people who used her agency were young and healthy. She'd had to deal with a few nervous breakdowns after a month on the bus, or near the end, after Gallipoli, the passengers not having contemplated before what it was like when the world was in uniform, or young men, to be precise, briefly in uniform, before they bled in their thousands into this earth. But this was different. She should get Hannah out of the office quickly; it might be unlucky.

Hannah withdrew her notice at work. Her boss was singularly helpful, considering that the office had by now been geared up for the arrival of her successor. He telephoned the putative new employee who said she understood – what else could she say? He also gave Hannah a week off, in all honesty because he thought, by the sound of things, that, well … After the week, she came back and got herself organised into a flawless rhythm. She slept at night, simply because she was too tired not to do so. In the morning she had a rushed breakfast. This was the most distracted time, the time she had to deliberately make herself not think about Simon in his bed, wonder if perhaps in the night some healing had occurred. She then took her normal train, did her normal morning's office work, and at lunchtime answered increasingly scarce questions about Simon's progress. She went out, had a short walk and bought her evening meal, something light. She would have it ready and with her, so as not to waste time in the evening by having to go to the shop. She would eat it either after getting off the bus, or on the seat inside the hospital gates. From work, she went directly there. It never occurred to her not to do so. Once or twice, friends asked her if she might not skip one evening and come out with them, but she said, 'Ah, no, I wouldn't like to.'

She did not say, 'This could be the day and it would be terrible if I wasn't there.'

'But we're going to the film club this evening, a Paul Cox film,' her workmate said.

'A Paul Cox film, oh.'

'Art house.'

That certainly put the evening a cut above the rest.

'We're going to a wine bar.'

These were new flash places that served only wine.

'There's one just opened in Crows Nest. Meg said there's a drink there called Cold Duck. She said it was lovely – would you not like to come?'

Eventually the friends stopped asking her. As the time went on and Simon still lay in his tranquil sleep, she decided to take one Sunday afternoon a month off. She visited the hospital briefly in the morning and then went to Cassie's house. Cassie had come out ten years before Hannah. She had married twice and was currently single.

'Look what I would have missed if I'd stayed at home. A decade of mistakes.'

And Cassie would laugh, opening whatever drink was to hand. The first time that she had got divorced, she carried the decree nisi document in her pocket for a few months. She didn't know what use it could be, but thought that she might find one. You should be able to find some use for a thing as big as that. She never did, so eventually put it in the drawer, where it now had another one to keep it company. After each divorce she had gone through her address book and scored out names. She told stories against herself continuously, and yet gave the impression that the laugh might be worth it. It was this nonchalance, pretended or not, that attracted Hannah in these particular times. She needed this kind of deceptively dismissive humour. Cassie did not ask too much about how Simon was now – what will be will be. But she did regularly ask about how Hannah and he had met. A love like hers, the persistence of holding the hand of a comatose person, surely deserved to be aired occasionally, Cassie thought. The telling never failed to animate Hannah. It would appear that the night they met everyone around them felt something, or so they said afterwards. They even said that you could tell immediately that they were made for one another. Made for this? Cassie wondered. She sometimes tried to get Hannah to look to the future, but mostly she allowed her to drink too much and sometimes to collapse into the spare bed. The next day Hannah would begin the routine again.

During Simon's convalescence, as Hannah optimistically referred to the state of affairs, she learned how to be patient and what the word meant. In the beginning she spoke to the other sick people's visitors, but that soon began to have its dangers. The futile stoking of hope had its awkward moments. It could sometimes become embarrassing because patients progressed or did not progress at different rates. It was difficult to strike the correct balance when there was an improvement or a deterioration at the neighbouring bed. And it was impossible to predict what each evening would bring. One man lived even though he had been hit by a road train; another died even though he had choked on a chicken bone.

It was during the fortnight when there was no other patient in the ward with Simon that Hannah decided she needed to do something for herself. But what? The empty beds (waiting for people who had not had their accidents yet), and the lack of visitors who were useful occasional diversions, all prompted her to wonder about her own time. The nurses dropped into the ward more often than normal during this fortnight, checking that she was all right. They lifted Simon's hand, squinted at the drips, as if all this might suddenly elicit a comment from him. Hannah thought that she might explain to one of them what she was feeling. But her conversation stuttered, she was made shy by their individual attention. And really, as she tried to explain, she realised that she didn't know what she was feeling. It would take more than one telling to clarify that. She decided that nurses do not need to use their imaginations – enough happens before their eyes. They do not need to know what's going on in the mind. In fact, in order to get on with the job, they specifically should not know. They need to get home, get the uniform washed and get down to forgetting, in whatever way suits. She resolved that, by the sixth month, if Simon was not home, she would begin something. She would have to find a thing with a new meaning. Even the nurses had begun to look at her with sympathy. One of them had tried to start a conversation about spare time and hobbies. Hannah had looked blankly back at her. The nurse had then said, 'Do you believe in God? Oh, sorry, sorry, I shouldn't have asked you that.'

'No, it's all right,' Hannah said, 'I didn't think I did but now I'm not so sure. But it's a big thing to be certain about.'

'Yes, of course,' the nurse said, and hurried away.

And it was Simon's lists, his collections, and his photographs of Yass and Gundagai that gave her the idea. She came across them accidentally, when she was looking for her passport. She had been asked for it at the bank: they needed all sorts of paperwork to allow her to shift money from the overland fund to the workaday joint account. The photographs were in one pile with a dozen or so cuttings, clipped to the outside. Why? Heaven knows. Simon did things like that. Now everything that Simon did was more interesting than it had been when he was doing it. She fingered the pictures. This was his present to her. There had been something about those places; she would find out what. If there was nothing much then her feelings were wrong. And there could be no harm in that. These were places she remembered well, better than many a road stop they had done. And if the visiting of them had started disturbed, in truth it had ended well. She remembered going back to the bedroom, where Simon was turning into his last web of sleep, almost waking, coming up to the day. She had taken off her clothes and got back into bed beside him.

At breakfast, when she had mentioned the church, the landlord had told them that was where the Irish girls had mostly got married. The ones that were brought over after the famine. Over a hundred to this region, they reckoned. Someone had just discovered the marriage register, he said. 'You'd think they'd have noticed before this. They have a wedding every ten years, then suddenly there's one every ten days and no one notices. Tea or coffee?'

Looking out the window of Simon's hospital room, Hannah wondered why no one had bothered to know. But then, she thought, this place is full of deliberately forgotten pasts. People have dropped their memories here. The place is full of people who have spent their time secretly remembering and secretly longing, then casting aside what has just come into their minds. And no sooner have that

165

crowd stopped, no sooner has the melancholy begun to recede, than another crowd comes to blow the bellows of memory again. You could be walking down any street here and not notice that people beside you have suddenly stopped dead in their tracks, puzzled. They have just had a sense of being out of place, truly, so far out of place. They put a hand out to touch something familiar, you bump into it. Both of you say, sorry mate. You want to say something else, because you're in a good and a perceptive mood, and you know what the look of lonesome is, but you don't. Because it's wise not to be too smart. You could be taken up wrong, the other person not yet having understood what has just happened them.

One evening Hannah arrived refreshed for her visit. She could never tell why the moods of the visits changed, not always in tandem with how she had woken, or what pleasant or unpleasant things had occurred during the day at work. It was as if she picked up her mood once she entered the foyer, picked it up as if it was a protective gown. It was a ghost of a gown and could not be dictated to. When she reached the ward there were three new patients, three new sets of stunned visitors. She watched them from the corners of her eyes. One woman bustled in to the far bed and placed a bundle of books on the locker.

'When he wakens up, he'll need some of these. He always reads books, never newspapers. That's the one he was reading before this, *Mr Darwin's Shooter*. Imagine that – *Mr Darwin's Shooter*.' She looked over at Hannah and dropped her voice to a whisper, 'Sorry, sorry, I'm being a bit loud. Is your husband sleeping?'

'No, it's all right,' said Hannah, wondering what life the woman was trying to create with only a bed and a locker, and of course the absent spirit. She decided not to answer the question – no need for the woman to know what could and couldn't happen here in this ward.

Hannah rubbed Simon's hand, placed it back on the bed and walked to the window. The rain had cleaned the air, then disappeared, performed a flash withdrawal as it could in this country. How could rain be so different to what she had grown up with? The sky above the harbour was on fire, begging for a twilight. But it would soon be dark, no gradual dimming of its splendour, just a sudden dropping into the sea. Maybe there would be stars on her way home, and she could look up into the sky, making new maps to go with the new stars that were now hers, no matter what she wanted. She left the hospital at her normal time, by her now familiar route, with her now established stoicism.

Hannah began her historical search almost immediately after the evening it had come to her mind. It was new. It was an after-accident pursuit. It was a diversion. It gave her things to write home about. And if they thought it strange, what did she care? She had lots of time to write letters now, after she got home from the hospital, and notes to herself and lists that were always lying about untorn, and lots of time to spend alone, too much, and she filled it with these new facts. What's so odd about that? Didn't people take up golf? They hadn't always played it. Didn't people decide to listen to opera, train themselves? Or study architecture, never having noticed the line of a street before, or start going to auctions? She would find out the stories of girls who had been brought to Yass, Gundagai and thereabouts; girls who had been brought without hope of ever returning to where their lives had begun. She would study these girls, move beyond just the genealogy of them; she would imagine them. After all, she had something in common with them. They could not go home. Nor could she now. Simple really. Not a long phrase. Easy to say. Let's not make an epic out of it. Maybe she would follow some of the ones who had ended up in Sydney; find what churches they'd married in and been buried from. That way she could drop in perhaps, between hospital visits, talk to them. Maybe that's what believing in God was. And if she got tired of them, she could go on to Mary Lee, the woman from Monaghan who had fought tooth, nail and back of a lorry for votes for women. And there would be other things, smashing stories, all lit up with the glow of history.

In the evenings Hannah now had something new to report to Simon. He would be much more interested in these stories, more than in office gossip, which could get tedious enough, and become flat in the retelling. And he would be proud of her meticulousness. It was while she was telling him one of the Aboriginal meanings of The Three Sisters, and about how she was a little like them now, unable to go back to her former self, that he moved his finger.

'You could if I got out of here,' Simon said, without opening his eyes. At least she didn't think he'd opened his eyes. Surely, she would know if that had happened. He had grey eyes, she thought, or green, they could look blue too. She'd forgotten. Oh God, she had forgotten the colour of his eyes.

Hannah shouted out for the nurses. They came and fussed and fussed and exchanged opaque glances with each other. Hannah was afraid that they would not believe her. The doctor came, 'Tell me again what he said. Exactly.' Hannah repeated the words.

'But that suggests that he knows where he is?'

'Well yes, maybe,' Hannah cried. She wept louder. 'You don't believe me.'

And then she screamed at Simon. After all the months, her patience deserted her. 'Speak to me, speak to me,' she screamed at him.

They took her outside and gave her tea.

'I don't want to be out here. In case it happens again.' If only a nurse or a visitor had been nearby. Oh well, what difference would it have made. Hannah insisted on staying with her head on the bed beside Simon's hand, and the nurses thought it best to allow her, just for tonight.

Hannah didn't think she nodded off, although a wisp of a dream kept doing nice things to her. And as the noise of the birds slipped in with the smell of dawn, Simon woke, and put his hand on the back of her sleeping neck, as if it had been there all the time. Hannah holds all the emotions of that day in every look she gives him, still. If she forgets, it's only a momentary lapse.

She sometimes said, 'So that's how I know so much about histories that have happened here. I'm very fond of those stories.'

And if she was asked, 'And how's Simon these days?' she said, 'Fine. Fine.'

If truth be known, he wasn't totally fine. But Hannah was entitled to her own deceptions. Sometimes she looked at the walls of their kitchen and thought, how strange, for a man who always knew which map came next, now he doesn't always know where he is himself.

The meeting between Hannah and Tara was not as awkward as might have been expected, blood apparently being thicker than lost time. Tara had finally been persuaded by all and sundry to go: 'Just once, someone has to visit her.'

Her boyfriend, Padraig, was away working, so her

brother Marcus had left her to the airport – no fear of him going to Australia but he did drive her out to the new terminal, which hid the old spiral building. He sauntered about Departures with the confidence of a person who only ever took short-haul flights and not often at that.

'I remember the day she went,' he said. 'I remember a fierce amount of crying.'

He helped Tara to check in her bags, waved a perfunctory goodbye, said, 'Enjoy yourself, don't look so glum about it, you'll be back in no time.' He could still kick on the shins, but Tara smiled. 'Yes, you're right, it's just this wasn't at the top of my list, it wasn't even on it. Still, off I go.'

And Tara gave herself over to the tyranny of long-distance travel, at first fighting with her body and her mind, then cajoling them to survive this journey together. The banking over Sydney was a mere prelude to being able to walk, although she did look with bleary eyes out the window. She wasn't sure what view she was seeing. It could wait. And she did, at long last, leave the aeroplane, suspended in half-asleep pleasure as she waited for her bags.

When she saw her cousin Hannah, Tara thought there was a confidence about her that she had not anticipated. She hadn't known that she had expected otherwise until she saw her. But then, what did she know about Hannah? In truth, nothing. Because if she had ever sent cards or letters, before the recent outbreak, Tara had well and truly forgotten. Maybe her mother had read them and talked about them, but Tara had certainly taken no interest, of that she was sure.

But the mothers must have talked about Simon, and the accident, and what it would mean for Hannah. They must have descended into a numb sort of grief together,

Hannah's mother more distracted than the others. The rest of them must have coaxed her along, stretched the piece of good news that she was clutching that day, elongated it out over hours, nurtured it until it seemed as if it might sprout wings. They must have dropped sentences carefully into the ruminations; it would never do to be too optimistic. That could be perceived as being patronising. Or worse still, as impatient. Yes indeed, Tara must have heard all those things bandied about. Yet it seemed to have passed her by, because here she was standing in front of Hannah and Simon, trying to remember exactly what had happened to him, and how his recovery was or wasn't coming along. She would have to wait and see. But how would she know? Perhaps she would mistake a mere eccentricity of his for an effect of the accident.

Hannah got her and the bags to the car and drove to their house, giving a running commentary on the obvious sights while Tara tried to keep her eyes open.

Simon looked at her dreamily. 'Your cousin, you say.'

After a shower and a glass of wine Tara felt resurrected. Hannah began her talking. Shockingly, she seemed to know everything about Tara. But a skewed everything – Tara's life as told by someone else, to someone else, ending up only half-recognisable.

'Your boyfriend's a landscape gardener. He'd do well here. What's his name? Padraig,' she said before Tara could reply. 'And youse go to Clare all the time,' Hannah said, lapsing into her language.

'I wouldn't quite put it like that,' Tara said. 'We occasionally go to Clare, and other places.'

'And you're very involved in amateur dramatics.'

'Well, I wouldn't quite put it like that.' She might have to stop saying that.

'And you were in Paris last May,' Hannah said dreamily. 'Imagine that, Simon. Imagine being able to go to Paris.' She got up abruptly from the table and muttered some emergency words about tea, trying to change the subject, as if she had just stepped on something dangerous.

'Where's Paris again?' Simon asked.

'France,' Hannah shouted from the kitchen.

'Of course,' Simon said.

Tara tried to imagine not knowing where Paris was.

'Here's your bedroom.'

Tara closed the door, overwhelmed with a desire to sleep, but Hannah knocked a few moments later and came in. 'Oh, it's great to see you,' she said, and stood looking at Tara as if she couldn't quite believe her. 'Sorry,' she said, 'later, when you've had a few hours sleep, we'll go to a party in my friend's house. Simon may or may not come with us. But I want you to meet my friends.' And Tara, suddenly, wanted to meet them too.

After a few hours Hannah woke her with a cup of strong coffee and ushered her into a taxi and over to the party. Simon might come. A neighbour, who was coming later, would pick him up if needs be. It was now eight o'clock in the evening, yet Tara felt as if she was going on a dawn ride. But when she had been led into the party she was wakened again by the ripple of expectation and satisfaction that was going on. A lot of introductions were made. Tara forgot the names almost immediately. The jetlag might have been to blame. Or there were too many people who looked exactly like people she knew at home. But they weren't them. She decided to cling to the kitchen, where food was being continuously brought in by more new arrivals.

And in time, Simon, who had indeed come in the end after changing his mind several times, joined her there. At first, he didn't seem to know who she was, but that didn't surprise her. And then he started telling her a rambling fantastical story, which might or might not have been true. Because the alternative was too bleak, she envied him the reality he appeared to have made for himself. He could not be held accountable for every 'I' and every 'T', and yet he did have the overall picture. He also had an uncensored sense of humour, which showed itself periodically. But maybe that was the effect that Australia had had on him, insofar as place changes one's humour, or maybe it was the accident, or maybe it had always been him.

'My wife—'

'Why do you always call Hannah your wife?'

'Because sometimes I forget her name and that's hurtful.'

'Oh, I see,' Tara said.

She remarked on the number of people who looked like exact replicas of people she saw every day, and how disconcerting that was. 'And I don't mean people who came here the same time as you.'

'We're a bit like the Children of Lir. Swans endlessly forced to roam. Although we don't have to stay three hundred years in each place. It was three hundred, wasn't it?'

'Yes, three hundred on Lough Derravaragh, three hundred on the Sea of Moyle, and three hundred off the Isle of Inish Glora.' Tara surprised herself; she would not have been able to remember that normally.

'And of course we cannot all sing. Be warned,' Simon said.

They stayed quiet for a while, an easy quiet. A woman beside them whinged a kind of envy at everything her companion said. And then she began to describe the bad qualities of her daughter.

173

'It's herself she's describing,' Simon whispered. 'Tell me about your new girlfriend,' he said to a man who asked him to move so he could find another carton of beer to put in the fridge.

'Well, she's a judge's daughter–' the man began, apparently humouring Simon.

'I didn't ask you about her father's job,' Simon said.

The man turned on his heel, disgusted.

'See what I mean?' said Simon.

Tara didn't, but nodded as if she did. Then he abruptly changed the subject again and she thought that she might get the swing of him yet.

'Did you know that self-awareness has gone mad? You can now say "I'm mean" and think, because you've explained yourself, it's acceptable to *be* mean.'

He then walked over to the bookshelf and took down a book on Australian trees and foliage.

'Look at this. You can tell your husband about this.'

'He's not my husband.'

'Doesn't matter. You can still tell him.'

So, they browsed through the tree book, looking at specimens that were totally alien to Tara. Simon turned the pages. 'This is called a grass tree.'

It looked like a hippy lamp to Tara.

'And this is melancholy thistle.'

'What's that?'

'You don't know what melancholy thistle is?'

'No, never heard of it. What is it?'

'Is he going to be your husband?'

'Who? Oh, Padraig. No. At least I don't think so.'

'Why?'

'I don't really like marriage. It's a bit smug.'

'Really,' said Simon, laughing.

And Tara wondered why on earth she'd said that, and if indeed she meant it.

'Do you like being married?' she asked him.

'I've never been asked that, so I'll have to think.'

She let him think for a while, annoyed now with herself for having got into a conversation that might disturb him.

'What's good about marriage is that if you get sick, the doctors talk to the person who matters to you most. Peculiar reason to get married. Will you marry me? I want to be the one to deal with the doctors when you're dying.'

Tara didn't know what to say, so turned another page of the book. 'Look at this one,' she said. 'Never saw anything like that before. It must be weird not being able to recognise the grass along the road.'

'It was the same with stars. I didn't know that I had ever noticed them until I looked up here one night and could find nothing that I knew. Of course, everyone says that.'

People drifted close but generally ignored them. They did sometimes offer to get Tara another drink and then passed the bottle speedily over Simon's glass. They offered a lot of plates to him. Simon winked, 'They're afraid to give me too much drink in case I'll forget some more.'

It was hard to know whether to laugh, or smile sympathetically. Or what to believe of him. It was as if he was in a state of suspense.

Hannah would occasionally bring people over. 'And this is my cousin,' she would beam again, each time her voice full of surprise.

'Oh great. I didn't know you had a cousin coming.'

'You didn't know she had any family at all,' Simon would say.

'Now Simon,' Hannah would say, and scurry off again, as if she had to do all the talking possible tonight, as if

Tara's presence, and the fact that she was conversing with Simon, had released her in some way. And yet, what did Tara know. Maybe she was always like this.

The guests began to come into the kitchen, collect their food containers, say goodbye and depart. When there were just a few people left, a large woman in the corner was persuaded to sing.

'It's okay,' Simon whispered, 'she can.'

She hummed her way into the first line, shifted her body and then sang 'Bessie the Beauty of Rossinure Hill' in a loud voice. But, although her voice was clear, people moved closer to her, as if they couldn't hear her from where they stood. They cocked their ears and looked like people who had never heard the song before, and might learn something that would help them live, if only they could get near the words. Tara thought it too unbearable. No matter where that song was sung, the words had too much loneliness in them. That was fine, if the listener was near Rossinure Hill or within checking distance of it. But here, it was dangerous. People might be thinking about the last time they had heard it, or the best time, or the worst time, or whose song they thought it was. She could see the deep concentration in their faces. Some people turned their eyes away from the longing in it, in case they drowned in sorrow. The listening was such an active thing you could imagine someone's memory getting stuck on a line, halfway through a verse, and never being able to move on. They could be found dead, heartbroken, lost in a song. At the finish there was a silence, to let the notes fade away. Then people applauded. The clap helped to shake the words off them. Then another voice began.

'Now wait until you hear this. Maybe you should cover your ears,' Simon said, too loudly. Hannah jumped up, and everyone began to help them get ready to go. The taxi was called and the three of them got into the back seat. Hannah and Simon held hands. Tara fell asleep.

In the morning, which was Saturday, Hannah took Tara outside to the table under the tree for breakfast. There was a heavy scent from the remains of the burned-out citrus sticks. An empty wine bottle lay languidly at an angle. Hannah picked it up and looked at the label before she put it in the bin. She then brought fried strips of thin bacon to the table. 'In honour of you,' she said, beaming.

Or was it perhaps in honour of herself. For having survived and not folded up, and for having finally got a member of her kith and kin to come here. She sat down and poured the tea. She ate quickly and rested her elbows on the table. She was greedy for family news, and Tara did her best, although sometimes she mixed up the cousins. She'd lost touch with most of these people, who seemed to Hannah to be immediate and frozen in time. Tara did not know if Eddie had died, or if he was still in hospital, or where he was buried, if he had died.

'You do know who Eddie is?' Hannah asked her.

'Yes, of course.'

Hannah looked at her doubtfully. 'I'm not always told about people being sick,' she said. 'I'm so far away it's pointless, I suppose.'

'Maybe you're lucky. People don't just tell you about sickness because you can do something. It's also a kind of warning. So, when you're away you can avoid that pessimism. When you're away you get told more about births, not deaths,' Tara said, longingly. And Hannah suddenly remembered the Scottish woman on the boat. She had tried to stay away from those with only bad news and although some had come to her unbidden it had not overwhelmed her.

Hannah jumped up to get her photographs, many of them of Ireland, old ones, ones with the shadow of herself in them, scarpering, playing too late on summer evenings, ones with the debris of her youth. There were present-day ones as well that must have been posted to her, including one of Padraig. 'That's your fellah, isn't it?' Tara couldn't remember the picture being taken and felt intruded upon. Then Hannah showed the pictures taken here, since she and Simon had arrived. Pictures of them as they were, but wouldn't know until later. They chronicled her mid-twenties, showing Australia mark itself on her face, her body, her clothes, the way she stood. The pictures of her and Simon in the beginning were surprisingly formal, becoming less so, and then jaunty. Before the accident. After the accident they showed what Simon was now. And yes, he had changed. But it was difficult to see in what way. Got younger maybe, while Hannah had aged, not in lines or body shape, but in a composed weight that had settled in her eyes, as she looked directly at the camera.

Hannah said, as she got up to go back to the kitchen to fill the pot, 'Tea in honour of you. Get your pictures – I'm dying to see them.'

Luckily Tara had brought a few. At the last minute of packing, Padraig had said, 'You'll need some photographs.'

Hannah examined them in detail, pored over them, saw each everyday thing in them, and handed them back. 'I'd forgotten that shade of paint,' she said.

Tara would look at them later in her room to see if she could see what Hannah saw. She lifted a book. 'Simon knows a lot of things about here, a lot of varied things,' Tara said.

'Yes, he knows a lot of new things. But you know he's forgotten that his mother has died,' Hannah said. 'I'm not sure whether that's a good thing or not. They sent me a dress of hers; I wore it to see would he notice anything. Nah. Not a thing. Maybe it's a good way to be.'

Tara could not think of a suitable reply. Probably best to say nothing.

'And perfume. They sent me perfume of hers too. Funny I remembered the things I liked about her when I put it on, but Simon didn't notice that either.'

Tara again said nothing.

Hannah had taken a week's holiday. The calendar was pencilled in. Tuesday was Gundagai.

'And Yass, of course.'

'Of course.'

'The girls? The girls I told you about?'

'Yes, I remember.'

Simon would come too. He was certainly not at a job this week, and no one had yet told Tara if he ever worked now. That might be one of the things continually referred to: 'We tried that but it didn't pan out.' He walked around the garden a lot, smiling, clipping the occasional bush. Inside, he took books, apparently at random, from their shelves, and passed them around like offerings to whoever happened to be close by.

Hannah and Tara ignored Simon as they got things ready for the journey. He followed Tara into her bedroom. He had a puzzled look as if trying to find something in his head. Often he thought that there was something rattling in there. He felt a glow. Presumably it was wrong to feel a glow about his wife's cousin. But then, since he'd been in hospital, he experienced many things that were out of kilter with everyone else. This could surely apply to morality as well. Sometimes he found himself carrying to conclusion thoughts that seemed new to him, but that he wasn't sure shouldn't have been squashed the instant that they came into his mind. Words that should not be used by grown-ups came back to him. Thoughts that needed to be kept to oneself tumbled out of him, sometimes at peculiar moments.

Hannah called out, 'Simon, come here and help me with this.'

'Of course,' he said, politely.

Simon remembered admiring a large expanse of the harbour, remembered experiencing some emotion about it. He remembered losing himself in the picture of it, and the red roofs, and the dense growth pushing up between the houses. He remembered turning around, for some reason, and then what seemed like a pin pricked his temple; a pin that shot stars, yellow jabs, strobes into his head. The lights danced to a deafening, non-musical sound. They were like a freezing kind of light. And then they went out. He remembered more pricks, all in the dark, and someone squeezing his hand. He could feel the touch of that squeeze, and wanted to touch it back, but it was too far away from him. And then he swam up out of a hole. He could feel himself getting new skin, as he got to the top of the hole. What was skin? There was someone he knew, looking at him. What was 'know'? He fell asleep, but not down the hole, more afloat on the top of it. And when he woke the next time, he knew the woman's name. And also his own. His mouth was dry.

The story that people told him of that year was ludicrous in the extreme. But he would pretend to believe them. He knew what it was to make things up. Often he began to tell a story and ended it as he would have wished it to be, rather than how he knew it was. That seemed a harmless enough thing to do. During his first month, he often felt physically beside himself. He repeated, 'I am beside myself with worry.' He said it many times to see what it meant.

There were other things. Keep your back to the wall and mind the buses. Rust never sleeps. Keep the show on the road. He tried to write some sentences, but found himself painting pictures in the letters. LOOK, with two eyes in each of the Os. And bed, a body sleeping with its head on the b and his feet on the d. He checked himself in the mirror. He knew himself from the inside, but had to verify the outside. He remembered his face. His memory was indeed filling in. Soon it would be a lake in his head. Hannah had good looks. And was a bit of fun, helped to keep the show on the road. In the mornings he thought, so this is health. I must mind it. He went walking. One awning a Sydney street doth not make. And larks and summer. Koalas need to be touched. And sometimes girls. Some girls more than others. Last night Hannah had said that she wanted to spend time with her friend Cassie. What did you buy when you spent time?

His memory returned to him in parcels. Floods of them one day, gushing into him. And then nothing. Small green fields. Going out to get the sheets, stiff with frost, from the clothes line before school. He would have been asked to do this. That, just that. Nothing to go with it. Who asked him? Where were the fields? A bird bathing in the house gutter, whispering, in comparison to birds here. Later, other birds on telegraph wires, swinging on them and filling the evening with noise. A man's voice telling him that they were getting ready for Africa. Who was the man?

He remembered meeting Hannah, for that was her name. It was the thing that bothered him most, that he might forget her name. Actually, he didn't remember meeting her as such, but remembered recently having met her. Feeling that his heart was sitting out beside him and that it might fall; buying aftershave. Yes, he remembered buying aftershave.

He couldn't write at first. He could spell words, verbally, and he knew that they were signs, but he couldn't remember the shape of the letters. This distressed Hannah more than other things. He knew when she was distressed. She didn't know that he knew this. And then after a lull, another part of his past would arrive. And it would distract her worry. He examined the arrived news with pleasure. But sometimes he got stuck with details that he was sure belonged to someone else. There was a man and his pregnant wife. They went dancing as often as they could, at the time that 'Living Next Door to Alice' was all the rage. The man divulged this to Simon. He said that he was always afraid that he would let this slip some day to their daughter, Alice, because then she would know that she had been named after a song they had danced to. Which would be particularly bad, because people now shouted out at the chorus, 'Alice, Alice, who the fuck is Alice?' Simon occasionally asked Hannah, 'Do we know anyone with a daughter called Alice?'

'Why are you always asking me that?'

'Not always. Only sometimes, it comes into my head. Never mind, it doesn't matter.'

And it didn't really, except that it would not be good to have someone else's memories.

Two months after Simon had come home from hospital his old boss telephoned. If Simon liked, he could come back to work to do some light office duties. Why not? he thought. He had been an insurance underwriter, he was told. He had been head of his department. He remembered nothing of insurance. When Hannah explained it to him, he thought it a bit like a card game. She told him about the layout of his office, what his normal day had been. He could imagine himself to the door, but then his memory cramped and wouldn't come out of the spasm.

'Never mind,' said Hannah, 'we'll see how it pans out. It's not a catastrophe if you can't remember insurance.'

Simon wondered if 'pan out' had anything to do with getting gold. 'Not a hanging matter,' he said, having heard someone say this in a shop, and having wanted to use it.

'Exactly. Not a hanging matter.'

'Did you telephone me when I was at work?' he asked.

'Yes, sometimes, although in my job at that time it was a bit hard to get time to make personal calls.'

'I see,' said Simon, not seeing at all, because he had forgotten what job Hannah had done at the time, and to be honest what job she did now.

On the morning of returning to work, Simon watched the colour of the dawn sliding up. Soon his window would be full of it. He was wet with perspiration so had his shower, but became wet again with the effort of drying himself. 'Maybe I'll just stand out the back and let the sun dry me.'

'Don't think that's a good plan,' Hannah said, trying to be full of patience but he could hear some annoyance in her. She was not amused. Sometimes he couldn't understand why some things amused her and others didn't; maybe it just had to do with time. Still, he wouldn't stand outside. She knew best. She drove him to work, even came to the tenth floor with him. On the way out of the lift he was ambushed by a smell and a sound, but he couldn't pinpoint what they were. His boss told him that Ross Parkes had been promoted to his old job, for the moment.

'But he's no good,' Simon said. Strangely, he knew for sure that Ross Parkes made mistakes when calculating.

How could he know that he was no good at insurance if he had forgotten what insurance was? Never mind. A vaguely familiar man stopped at a desk and said to the woman making notes, 'He doesn't mean anything.' I know that, thought Simon, I know what it is not to mean anything. I am the only person here who knows what it is not to mean anything. Even to myself.

'Welcome back.'

'Thank you.'

Simon spent a pleasant few hours filing, putting things in alphabetical order. It was good for his spelling. Someone would double-check later.

'You can go home now. Hannah is waiting for you.'

Hannah would come to collect him at lunchtime for the first week. They would see how it worked out.

'Is it okay with your work?' Simon asked.

'Oh yes. One of the others will cover for me. It's just a little difficult because I'm only in the job six months.'

'Oh, not long then.'

'Yeah. And I do love it, so I don't want to mess it up.'

Now was his chance. 'What do you like most about it?'

'Well, organising someone's overland holiday from the very word go. Imagining the distance that they will be travelling. I prefer that to just booking flights. We do have some plane hopping as well, though mostly it's straight through, with maybe a night's stopover.'

'Look, the jacaranda is going purple,' Simon said.

'I didn't think we had jacarandas in Sydney. I thought they were only in Queensland. Are you sure?'

'No, I'm not,' Simon said, but not sadly.

He was tired, as if from a hangover, and went to bed in the afternoon. He could feel himself fading away into sleep. And he didn't waken until it was almost dark. He looked out the window and the sun had fallen halfway down between two trees.

Hannah came home late. By then Simon had recovered from the gloom of the afternoon sleep. But when the door slammed, he jumped and missed a minute. That often happened, him missing a whole minute, as if a crack had opened in his brain. What happened in the world, he wondered, when he was gone? But he now knew that if gave a low moan more of his memory would come back when the missed minute was over. He had been able to explain this to Hannah. She heard the moan. This is going to work out, she thought.

And a month after that it had been decided to take Simon on a short aeroplane journey. Hannah had organised this from work. He was happy to go along. They trundled out to a far end of Sydney airport, past the monstrous jets, some of which were revving up in preparation for their lift into the sky. It was important to remember that if you threw a hat into the wind it did not fall, it caught on the current and flew by itself. Hadn't something done that to him? There. They walked out to the small plane. The hold was being loaded.

'What's in the bags?' Simon asked.

'Letters.'

'How strange. I thought letters came on trains and ships. And where am I being posted?'

'Ha!' Hannah laughed, taking his hand as they walked up the steps. But when they got to the door Simon leaned over and whispered urgently, 'Hannah, Hannah, Hannah.'

'Yes. What is it?'

'I don't want to go into there. I can't. I'd never want to go in there.'

Panic oozed from him and the strength in his hand, as

he pulled her back, was remarkable. 'Okay,' Hannah said, 'that's all right, we won't go. Don't worry, no one will make you, we won't go.'

But a look of utter desolation passed over her face, as if a black cloud had worked its heavy way over her entire being. 'There's no point,' she said briskly to the pilot. 'Another time, maybe.'

She turned quickly, faced the departure lounge and walked ahead of Simon, for one brief minute overcome with rage against her luck. Not against him, against her luck. She knew that she could not manage him on the long ship journey; an aeroplane had been her only hope. She would have to start asking her family to come here or she would forget faces the way he had forgotten words. It might take years to convince them.

The beginning of the journey home was silent and heavy, until Simon said, 'Did you know that a nosegay is a bunch of sweet-smelling flowers?'

Hannah now had a drawer of her own in the front room. Simon couldn't remember her having that before, but was aware of his unreliability in these matters. She had charts of names, some unfamiliar; books and articles and photographs and stories about myths, all neatly divided with paper clips and rubber bands. Such tidiness. Such history. He would read these things. Perhaps in the search through all these things of Hannah's he could fill in his own past. He was in a hurry to do that, eager for clues. He found nothing in them for himself, but plenty about other people, people come to this land, in the permutations of the multiplication of people that they had started. That's when you know for certain that you have had intercourse – when your grandchildren start to write with wonder about you

Simon was very taken by intercourse at the moment. Hannah had held his hand a lot when he had come home from hospital. And sometimes rubbed him when they were in bed. It was pleasurable and gave her a distant dreamy look. Then one morning she had come back to bed, showered and perfumed; she looked very dressed although she had no clothes on. She rubbed him as she had been doing for months now, but there was more of an urgency to this. She deep kissed him, that's all he could call it. And it was this, the wet communion, that sent ripples through him. It was as if Hannah was doing his breathing for him. He was a little taken aback. But he followed her, and was soon in the throes of an exquisite experience, lost in a vortex of extreme electrical pleasure. It was hard to believe that such a thing could be. When they were lying together he looked at Hannah. Her face glittered with light, as if decorated with thin strips of tinsel. He wondered how he could have forgotten that. Sex, she called it, but he found the word intercourse and liked the formality of it better. He liked the way they could come back to it if they felt like it and remember it if they didn't.

It was after an evening in which Simon had asked Hannah about those notes in her drawer that she decided to write the letter home.

'I wonder what Vincent Van Gogh wrote to his brother Theo in all those letters. It's peculiar to write to a brother so much. Unless he was in jail of course. Or sick or something,' Simon said.

Hannah would ask for someone, anyone, to visit. Outside, in the dark, the cars were making distant noises as they sloshed through unexpected rain. Shadows of broken-up yellows fell on the corners as the rivulets of water streamed down streetlights, blotting what should have been unbroken reflections. Hannah would have to believe in this letter.

'I'll pay the fare,' she wrote.

'There'll be no need for that,' her mother wrote back. 'We think Tara might go.'

Tara worried about the morning of her leaving to return home. She had begun to feel an unexpected excitement at going back to her life, but thought it would be rude to let that out. She made no fuss about packing her bags. In the end it was all fine.

'We'll leave Simon at home,' Hannah said, as she got ready to go to the airport. 'Best to say goodbye to him here.'

Tara didn't quite know how to do this but in the end simply said, 'Well, I'll see you.'

'I don't think so,' Simon said. 'Do I have cousins, Hannah?'

At the departure gates Hannah said, 'Thanks for coming. I did need to see someone, but I'm all right now. Don't cry.'

She thought that it had been a good visit. She was attached again. Now that she had seen someone from that faraway part of her life, maybe she would come up with a plan for a new way of living, if there could be one. Or maybe not.

Tara turned once to wave goodbye and then resolutely kept walking. Hannah sighed. Maybe she would go see Cassie; she hadn't seen her in an age. Yes, that's what she would do, go see Cassie.

ACKNOWLEDGEMENTS

I am indebted to Monaghan County Council and to Wakefield Press, Adelaide, for assistance given towards research into the life of Mary Lee. For aiding travel to various literary festivals, which journeys always double up as fact-finding projects, I would like to thank Culture Ireland. Thanks to the Arts Council of Ireland for their ongoing support. Appreciation goes to Frances Stonor Saunders for her book *The Woman Who Shot Mussolini*. The story 'Two Gallants Getting Caught' was first published by Tramp Press in *Dubliners 100* as a response to Joyce's original, celebrating one hundred years since publication.

Thanks also to the Tyrone Guthrie Centre at Annaghmakerrig for their exchange programme residency at the National Writers' House, in Varuna, Australia, and to the Ireland Funds for a residency at the Princess Grace Library in Monaco, both of which were a tremendous help in progressing work.

Earlier versions of some of these stories have been published by The Stinging Fly; New Island Press; Tramp Press; Tratti, Italy; Ecnu Press, China; and Accenti, Canada.

My thanks to Sean O'Reilly, Judith Gantley and Gerry Dukes for reading. Also to Fintan Vallely for continuing to keep me guessing.

My sincere thanks to editor Patsy Horton and publicist Jacky Hawkes, with whom it was a pleasure to work.